A ROSE MCLAREN MYSTERY

A GAME OF MURDER

LIZA MILES

Dedication

To mystery lovers and bakers everywhere and, in memory of my favourite Miss Marple.

The fabulous Joan Hickson OBE 1906-1998

Acknowledgements

My sincere thanks to Mary Turner Thomson, editor, and cover design, whose hard work, and attention to detail makes sure that I am always well dressed!

"Writing without revising is the literary equivalent of waltzing gaily out of the house in your underwear."

Patricia Fuller

Amy MacDonald, Muffin maker extraordinaire, who whipped up a delicious batch of Trixie's Festival Muffin. The recipe is at the back of the book.

Chapter One

Trixie felt puffed with pride as she totted up the profits from the day's takings. The idea for the mobile muffin and cake stand had taken several enthusiastic discussions to convince Rose it was worth the extra investment, but halfway through the first week of The Edinburgh Fringe Festival, she was already financially ahead. She had finally managed to blot out the events and thoughts that troubled her from two years ago.

"Ye're lookin' pretty pleased with yersel, hen," said Rob, mimicking Trixie's accent as he passed her on his way to play at a Fringe event.

Trixie pulled a face and held up a wad of Scottish bank notes. "Och ye of little faith Rob."

"Nah Trixie, I always believed in you. Coming to hear me and the band?"

"Aye wish ah could but ah've got batters tae mak' for th' morra. Hope it goes well. Expecting a fair crowd?"

Rob shrugged, "It wasn't bad last night, but after expenses I'm guessing we made about ten quid each."

"Och well ah hope ye dae better th' night." Trixie watched Rob disappear into the mass of people. The

Edinburgh Festival grew bigger every year, with performers from all over the world participating, as well as a huge international audience. She felt alive from the buzz of the crowd heading to a multitude of Fringe shows. She had sold out of pretty much everything except for the boxes of biscuits. The Festival Muffin, chocolate with raspberry sauce, had sold out first, another Trixie invention. It had taken several tries to get the recipe right, but the fudgy brownie texture with the raspberry filling was a winner. Rose had been worried it was too much like a brownie to call it a muffin, but the shop regulars who had taste-tested persuaded her, and Trixie's Festival Muffin was launched.

"Night," she called across to her neighbouring stall holder as she made her way to North Bridge and the top of the marble steps, on the walk back to Morrison Street. The Scotsman Steps, linking the old and new parts of Edinburgh, had reopened last year. Transformed from a dilapidated and dangerous blight on the city, they had formed part of an art commission, bringing art out of the galleries and onto the streets. Trixie usually loved walking on the different layers of coloured marble. Tonight though, as she turned the corner she saw an empty vodka bottle and then the figure of a young man wearing blue jeans and a dark hoodie lying on his front across one of the marble steps. She was reminded of earlier times. Trixie called out, then stepped to one side, making her way around him to the steps below. She had learned from experience, getting too close to a collapsed drunk can mean ending up with a black eye. Yet, despite the vodka bottle, the young man didn't look like an inebriate.

"Hey pal, are ye awright?" She stood and waited to see if there was a response. "Hey pal," she called again, louder this time. Again, there was no response. Trixie stared at the prone body. He didn't seem to be moving, and she couldn't hear any grunts or snorts that usually went with passing out from too much booze. She leaned in and decided to prod his leg. Nothing.

A young couple were heading up the stairs when they saw Trixie bending over the man. They immediately changed their minds and went back.

"Hey, Ah dinnae think he's that well, can ye help?" Trixie called after them, but they had vanished by the time her words were out. She pulled out her phone and called Rose. There was no answer. Trixie hesitated, she knew she couldn't just leave him there, but she wanted to run, not get involved, like she had the last time.

"Are you aright?" A man's voice called out. Trixie hadn't heard him coming down the steps towards her.

"Naw, he's nae movin'."

"Let me see." The man edged his way past until he was on the same step as Trixie. He tried for a pulse.

"Use your phone. We need an ambulance. I think he's alive, just. But I'm not a medic."

Trixie pressed 999, her hands were shaking. Once she had made the call it took forever for emergency services to arrive because of the crowds and the location. Trixie couldn't sit still as they waited. She was cold, despite the warm evening. The man with her unbuttoned the top of the black floor length cloak he was wearing and offered it to her. But Trixie refused the gesture.

"Thanks, but I dinnae think it will make a difference. It's in ma' bones. It's nae that baltic after all."

He nodded. "OK. Well, they should be here soon; I hear sirens at least."

Trixie and the man stood close to the wall above the poor soul as the ambulance crew made their way up the stairs, followed by two uniformed police. Within seconds he was loaded onto a stretcher. As they lifted him, a playing card fell from his pocket. Trixie went to catch it.

"Don't touch it!" One of the officers shouted at her, making her jump.

"Sorry."

The card fell face up. It was an arty version of the Queen of Spades Trixie hadn't seen before. It didn't seem to go with the young man in jeans and hoodie with well-worn sneakers now covered in a grey blanket and being carried down to the ambulance. The officer picked up the playing card and placed it in a plastic bag.

"Was this bottle here as well? Did you touch it?" The officer pointed to the empty bottle of vodka two steps below them.

"Naw, ah didnae touch it, and aye, it wis here. Just like that, with the cap off when ah came."

"What time was that?"

Trixie shrugged and looked at the man. "Aboot five minutes before he came. I called 999 a few minutes after."

"Alright, around five minutes before 6 o'clock then. Do you agree with that, sir?"

"Yes, that's about right," the man nodded. "Can we go now?"

"Yes, but in case we need to speak to you both again, where can we contact you?"

Trixie and the stranger gave their details to the police.

"So, you don't know each other?"

"No," they said in unison.

Afterwards, as Trixie made her way back to Muffins on Morrison, she realised she hadn't taken in the stranger's name or where he was from. He seemed curious about who she was, almost as nosy as she expected the police to be about someone finding an almost dead body. He'd invited her for a drink to settle her nerves, but there was something about him. That cloak he wore was creepy for one thing. She shuddered at the thought of putting it on. She hoped the man they had found on the steps would make it, and that her call had given him a chance to live. She felt numb. Rose was still working in the back kitchen of the shop when Trixie arrived, she was pouring batter into muffin cups.

"How did you get on? Another good day?" Rose called as she heard Trixie unlock the front door and make her way into the kitchen, "Sorry I missed your call. I was on the loo. Oh, heavens to Betsy Trixie, what on earth has happened?

Trixie was pale, her breathing was irregular as if she were about to faint. She dropped the bags she had been carrying and moved forward towards Rose. Rose grabbed her quickly and guided her into the shop where she could sit down.

"I'll get some water. Stay there. Keep your head on the table."

Trixie sipped the water slowly as she told Rose what had happened. “It reminded me o’ ...”

“Sorry Trixie, I can see it’s really shaken you up. But at least you were able to call for help. And he’s alive.”

“Och, when they loaded him onto the stretcher, ah thought about Dr Reynolds, after ye found oot he was run over and then murdered at the hospital, everything flashed through ma’ mind, as if it was all happening again.”

“Oh Trixie, I'm sorry. Look, why don’t you come and stay over at my place tonight? I’ve already prepped the batters and there’s enough to see us both through the morning, Rob can deliver some fresh stock to you at lunchtime. OK?”

“Are ye sure? Thanks. Ah dinnae think ah want tae be alone.”

“Yes, of course, we can watch a film, something funny perhaps. We could both use some cheering up.”

Trixie nodded. Maybe this would be an opportunity for Rose to talk to her about what was on her mind too. She had been out of sorts for the last few weeks. But Rose had snapped at both Rob and Trixie when they had asked if she was alright, what was bothering her. They hadn’t really talked properly, other than shop business, since February – now she thought about it since Rose had come back from the skiing holiday with Sarah. Sarah had vanished from Rose’s life as quickly as she had seemed to enter it.

It was after that holiday Rose had moved flats. Despite redecorating and moving furniture around, the ghost of Gary’s brother lying dead on her bed two years earlier had never left. Her new flat in Corstorphine was a tad further from Morrison Street, but peace of mind more than made up for the additional distance.

Rose had invested in two electric bikes, one for her for the commute and one with a covered wagon style trailer for Rob to make deliveries. Rose's green efforts had become quite a focal point for her business and the shop had been featured in the Edinburgh Evening News and on television.

"Will you manage the bike Trixie, we can get a taxi if not."

"Nae, I'll be guid, Rob willnae be pleased wi' me on his bike though."

"Haha, true he thinks he's king of the road after that picture of him in the paper went viral. *The Kilty muffin man*."

"Ye should use it Rose, they tourists, here for the festival, could buy it as a postcard wi' the biscuit boxes."

"Rob's head is big enough, he doesn't need me to puff him up anymore, especially now he's playing at the festival."

"He's no making money though, sae he'll be guid for deliveries for a while yet."

They set off on the bikes, Trixie's mood had shifted with the banter and by the time they arrived at Rose's flat, the boy she had found on the stairs was almost, but not quite, forgotten.

Rose learned the news of his death from DCI Chatterton the following afternoon.

"I'll come with Trixie to see you once we're closed, is that alright? She was in quite a dither last night. It brought everything back, you know, the other murders." Rose said, as she boxed up some muffins for the inspector to take with him. "But this isn't like that, right?"

"No, it seems like a horrible accident, he must have tripped, one of the laces on his shoe was loose. I'll know more once the pathologist has done her work, but we need statements and, well because of what happened before, I thought Trixie might find talking to me might be easier. It's unfortunate for her that she was the one to find him."

"And the other man? She said there was a man in a cloak who told her to call the ambulance. He seems to have creeped her out a bit. It was the cloak, I think."

"Yes, him too, although he's checked out of the hotel.

"Thanks for the muffins Rose. Here." He handed her some cash. "What's bothering you?"

"Mmmn, well just why the man checked out of the hotel. It seems odd."

"Rose, this was an accident, pretty sure, remember our agreement?"

Rose smiled. "Yes sir, promise, I won't interfere." As soon as the DCI left the shop Rose sent Trixie a text.

DCI Chatterton has just been in. I need to talk to you about that boy from last night, meet back here at 5? Everything OK at the stall?

Yeah, Rob delivered and it's slower than yesterday. The boy? What's happened?

Don't worry, I'll explain later. Do you remember the hotel that man was staying at?

I think he said The Belvedere. Why?

Nothing. See you later.

Rose put out the fresh muffins and cleaned up the sitooterie table. Like Trixie she had found business slower today and wondered if the fresh baking would be wasted. She checked on google maps for The Belvedere. It was just off George Square, a fancy boutique hotel in one of the Georgian houses with a five-star rating. Rose hadn't heard of it before, it was, according to the write up, exclusive and discreet. She pressed the call now button on their website.

"Hello, just calling about a customer, who left a book here in my shop. He mentioned he was staying with you, late thirties, wearing a cloak?" Rose drummed her fingers as the receptionist placed her on hold with the inevitable badly recorded classical music. Poor Vivaldi thought Rose as winter from the four seasons crackled in her ear. "Oh, OK thank you, did he say which hotel he was moving to, or leave a forwarding address so I can get the book back to him?"

The receptionist told Rose she wasn't allowed to share any information about guests, and she was sure that, if the book was important, their guest would return to collect it from her shop himself. Rose tried one more angle. "And, sorry you said his name, but I didn't write it down, can you tell me again? But the receptionist didn't fall for her trick.

"I didn't state the guests name," she replied coldly.

"Thank you. Well let's hope you're right and he comes back for his book. Bye for now."

Annoyed that the subterfuge hadn't worked, Rose hung up. That was that. She typed the name of the hotel back into her phone to see if someone had left a recent review, and if a name came up. But her investigation was swiftly interrupted, as a gaggle of hungry tourists arrived. She was busy for the rest of the day and by the time Trixie arrived, all the baking had been sold.

"What about the boy?" Trixie asked as the last customers left and she flicked the sign on the door of the shop to closed.

"I'm sorry Trixie, the DCI needs a statement from you. Apparently, the boy died. The DCI didn't say how, just that he thought it was an accident."

The colour drained from Trixie's already fair complexion, she nodded her head slowly. "When they put him on yon stretcher, ah just ken, somehow, that he wid die."

Rose pulled her in for a hug. "Come on Trixie, let's get the statement done, I said I'd go with you."

Trixie spent over an hour painstakingly trying to recall every detail before she was satisfied with her statement. The DCI was patient with her, his avuncular tone encouraging her to describe what she could remember as clearly as possible.

"Dae his family ken?" She asked.

"No, we haven't managed to reach anyone there yet."

"There?" Rose asked.

"Canada. He's from Canada."

"Och maybe that's why the playing card looked sae different, I havnae seen one like that before."

"Playing card?" asked Rose.

"Aye, the one that fell, when they put him on the stretcher. It was the Queen of Spades."

"We think it was part of his magic act - apparently he was here performing," said DCI Chatterton.

"Whit wis his name?" asked Trixie.

"Devon, but he performed as Card Shark. He had given a performance at The Scotsman earlier, and he was due back later. Full house and very popular apparently. Anyway, thanks Trixie, I'm sure we won't need to bother you again."

Trixie and Rose looked at each other as they walked out of the station. They both had the same ominous feeling, that this was definitely not the last time the DCI would be talking to Trixie about Devon.

Chapter Two

Rob had been ecstatic when his band managed to get a spot at Underbelly. "Made it, Rose," he whooped.

Watching him performing on stage, Rose was proud of her friend. The venue was packed, he had to be doing better than he was claiming. As the act finished Trixie put her fingers in her mouth and whistled.

"Aww he's really guid Rose, I had nae idea."

"Yeah, he had some bad luck when he played before. It's a pity. I think he could have made a name once."

"It's nae tae late, he's nae that auld Rose."

Rose laughed, "I suppose not, perhaps it's just because I turned thirty-seven last month that I'm beginning to feel middle aged."

Trixie winked, "Well ye could still pass fer younger."

Rose thought about that, she might not look her age but looks might not be an issue for her for much longer. She wasn't ready to talk about it yet, but the vision in her one good eye was getting worse. The last few months had been tough. The worsening eye and the break up with Sarah had brought her close to the brink of relapse, but thankfully, with the support of her sponsor, she hadn't gone there. Sarah had been a mistake, Rose had known that almost as soon as she had agreed to go on holiday with her. It was too soon after the trauma of the murders and she was trying to work things out with her father, now she wondered if she ever would. They had made progress, met at least, but when he found out about Sarah he shut her out again, his parting words, "Your mother will be turning in her grave," had stung.

"So, whatdyathink?" Rob joined them, jolting Rose out of her reflectiveness.

"Well done", she said. "Drinks on me - juice, tea, fancy coffee ... ?"

"Not here," said Rob, "too expensive, I've found a really cool place, follow me ladies, lassies, laddies."

"Is that ye tryin' tae be all PC Rob? Cos you missed out womin', and that's what ah am, a womin, nae a lassie." Trixie teased as she skipped along behind him. But as suddenly as she started the banter she stopped. "Rose, that's him, the man frae last night."

Rose followed the direction of Trixie's finger. "Where Trixie?"

"Och, where's he gone? He wis still wearin' that cloak."

"Maybe he's performing here. Let's go that way, see if we can find him and speak to him?"

But hard as Trixie scanned the crowd she couldn't see him again, he had vanished."

"Who are you looking for?" asked Rob.

Trixie told him what had happened the night before and about giving her statement to DCI Chatterton.

"Wow, that's really sad. I heard about Card Shark, he was getting good reviews."

Trixie and Rose looked at each other.

"Actually, do you both mind if we take a look in, at The Scotsman, I have an idea," said Rose.

"Rose? What are you doing?" asked Rob.

"Nothing, just ..."

"Putting things together and making a map," Rob interrupted.

Rose pulled a face at the reference to their joint efforts two years ago to solve who had murdered Rob's lover and the others. "It's just a thought, I mean have you ever tripped over your laces Rob, since you were grown up, I mean."

"Well, no, but it could happen. Stop looking for things that aren't there or, if they are there, are none of your business."

Rose put her head on one side, "Are you coming?"

Rob sighed, nodded and nudged Trixie, "You?"

"Och, why not. After all whit harm can it dae?"

The audience who had booked tickets for the room at The Scotsman, where Card Shark would have been performing the day before, were waiting to be let in as Rose, Rob and Trixie arrived. Another group of performers in costume and make-up, ready for an outside performance, were coming up the steps where Trixie had found the young man unconscious. There were people everywhere, and a queue of customers waiting for a table in the hotel's restaurant, The Brasserie, had spilled out onto the street. Rose looked around, if someone wanted to push someone down the steps it would be risky, but no one would take notice of one person helping another who was perceived to be in their cups.

"Trixie, how long do you think he'd been lying on the steps when you found him?"

Trixie shrugged, "Ah really dinnae ken."

"And the vodka bottle, what size was it, large, small?"

"Oh, one of them quarters. It was empty, but well he dinnae look like a boozer if ye know whit ah mean."

Rose nodded, "Well between us, we probably know what to look for, and if that's what you think Trixie, I'm inclined to believe you."

"And ye ken, the DCI, he said it wis a trip, nothin' tae do wi' drink."

"Yes, but then something doesn't add up. Why was the bottle left there like that? Let's see what time Card Shark's show finished and where he would have changed. If he was a magician, where were his props? Look, you two go and watch the show that's just starting, see where the performer enters from and exits, anything about the set-up. I'll go and chat with some of the staff. See you back here afterwards." Rose took £10 from her purse and handed it to Rob. "For the hat."

Rose knew a couple of the staff who worked at the hotel, they were regular customers at her shop, but neither of them were on duty and her attempts to engage the reception staff in conversation got her nowhere. She was about to try the bar staff when she saw a man in a cloak coming out of one of the lifts restricted for hotel guests. If he was a performer, he had to have money, most of the visiting acts would be sleeping on couches or at cheap hostels, not fancy hotels like this one or, if it was the same man Trixie had met the night before, The Belvedere. Rose followed him into The Brasserie. He went straight to the bar and took the only vacant seat. Rose took out her phone to try and get a picture to send to Trixie, she didn't want to waste time on the wrong person. But the wrong person for what, she wondered, just because if it was him and he had changed hotels, why did that bother her so much? Why didn't she accept the boy's fall had been simply the accident the DCI said it was? Trixie sent back a thumbs up.

"Nice cloak" said Rose, as she sidled up beside the man. "Performing?"

He moved his eyes to the side before turning his head and taking her in, clearly appreciating her look. "Yeah, first time here."

"Where are you performing?"

"Just free fringe, next year I'll make a better plan. It's tough to attract the audience, with so much competition. Here." He pulled out a printed promotional flyer from inside the cloak. "I can hide lots in this," he laughed.

His act was called 'Who am I' and he claimed to be the world's best impersonator of historical men.

"That's pretty unique, especially as most of us won't know what they sounded like anyways."

"That's where you're wrong." He replied. "You know most of us do have an idea, from the way they wrote, or what has been written about them. I do a good job, you should come, if you fancy it."

"Must be well paid if you can afford to stay here or at The Belvedere." Rose threw in the comment, hoping it would unsettle him, but he just smiled.

"Well let's just say I won't be giving up the day job, that's what pays for this. He circled his hand around the room."

"So, what's that then. The day job?"

"Can I get you a drink? My names Chris, Chris Foley." He held out his hand to her.

"No, you're alright, thanks. I don't." Rose looked down, suddenly embarrassed by her own behaviour."

"Coffee, tea? I'm a harmless history prof and writer, an academic, I suppose you would say."

"Well good luck with the show, I will come along, with a couple of friends. Sorry I bothered you." Rose pulled her jacket around her, what had she been thinking? Rob was right, she was making things up that didn't exist, but she could see why Trixie had been unsettled by the cloak Moments later, as she stood outside The Brasserie, updating her business page on Facebook waiting for Rob and Trixie to come out of the show and confess her mistake, she didn't register that the penetrating screams in the background were not from a performance. It was only when the people around her started saying "Oh my god" and "how terrible" that she realised something was going on. She looked up and saw four paramedics running past her towards a woman in costume covered in blood lying in the road. Another woman, the one who had been screaming was kneeling next to her. She was dressed as Alice in Wonderland.

Chapter Three

Rose watched as the paramedics did their work, but it looked as if whatever had happened to the woman had been fatal. Rose gasped as she watched them cover her face with a blanket. The police arrived, pushing back the crowd, and asking for witnesses. The party atmosphere had changed from gaiety to fear in seconds. It was as the crowd moved back that something on the ground caught Rose's attention and she walked over to it. It was a playing card, the Queen of Hearts. It was close to the body, but not within the parameters of the scene. She moved closer and straddled the card, trying to protect it from being trampled underfoot. As she looked down at the image, she noticed it was unusual. Trixie had described the card she had seen falling from the man on The Steps as arty. This one looked like that too. Could they be from the same pack? Rose took out her phone and took a photograph before waving at one of the police and drawing his attention to the card. The young officer shrugged. "No, really." she urged him. "This might be important, the man who fell and died yesterday on The Scotsman Steps, he also had a playing card."

The officer beckoned to one of his older colleagues and explained what Rose had told him. "I'll bag it then. Thanks, er Miss?"

"McLaren, Rose McLaren. DCI Chatterton will know who I am."

"I'll still need an address, did you see who dropped it?"

"No, sorry. I noticed it when the crowd moved away. I don't have good eyesight, but the colours are vivid so it caught my attention."

"You say you saw another playing card yesterday?"

"Not me, my assistant, she'll be here soon, but she gave a full account to DCI Chatterton, and you already have that card. It was the Queen of Spades."

As if on cue Trixie and Rob came over to Rose. "Whit's going on?" asked Trixie.

Rose shook her head and put her arm around Trixie.

"Trixie, does that card look like the one you saw yesterday, I mean the style?"

The officer held the bag up for Trixie to see.

"Aye, it does."

"Thank you," said the officer, noting down Trixie's contact information and details about where she had been, what she had seen when she came out of the show.

A small tent was being erected over the body of the woman. The ambulance had finally managed to get through the crowds on the blocked off street and park outside The Scotsman. Two paramedics were supporting the woman dressed as Alice into the back There was blood on the white apron of her costume, from where she had been kneeling over her friend.

“So did you see whit happened Rose?” Trixie asked.

“No, I was updating the business page, when I realised something was up, then I saw the card. It was far from the body, but it seemed important, because of the one you saw yesterday.”

“I wonder why it wis laying sae far away frae the body?” said Trixie.

Rose considered the question and looked at the distance between the tent and where they were now standing. “Do you mean because yesterday the card was with the boy, in his pocket?”

“Aye.”

“Well, if that was the intention, something must have gone wrong. Perhaps the person who hurt her thought they had been spotted. I mean, the two women were obviously together, it was a risky attack, to think you wouldn’t be seen. Yet no one seems to have seen anything, or anyone running away from the reaction of the crowd. Not until afterwards, when she was already dead.”

Rob scratched his head. “Like an illusion you mean. When you only see what you are meant to see.”

“Exactly” said Rose, “like the boy on the steps yesterday.”

“You’re convinced that his death wasn’t an accident?”

“Yes” said Rose.

“And he was here again, the man I saw yesterday, the one in the cloak?”

“He was, but he was inside The Brasserie Trixie, he didn’t come out, I’m sure of that,” said Rose.

"Perhaps that wis an illusion too. Did you have a wee chat wi' him?"

"I did, he's performing. Beyond the Fringe, he's a professor. Look, this is what he is doing here," Rose showed Rob and Trixie the flyer. "I could really use that coffee, shall we go back to mine, or the shop?"

"Sorry Rose, I have a date. I said I'd be there by now. Can we raincheck though? I'll see you on Tuesday if we don't speak before," said Rob.

"Ye're a sly fox," said Trixie, "Enjoy an' dinnae get yersel intae too much bother."

Rob laughed, hugged them both and took off down The Scotsman Steps.

Trixie shuddered, "Mind if we dinnae go that way, Rose?" She nodded towards the steps.

"Of course Trixie, the longer way is fine with me after everything that's happened."

It was gone ten by the time Rose got back to her flat. She and Trixie had decided to stop in on a cafe and eat as well. Trixie clearly hadn't wanted to talk about what had been happening so Rose was left with her own thoughts about what she had seen earlier, wondering who the woman was and how her death was connected to the boy on the steps the night before. The playing cards were hard to ignore as a factor in both deaths. She hadn't been a poker player, even in prison, where cards had been one of the ways to pass the time. She wondered if there were any clues in the cards that had been left. Together, the deaths were almost a macabre piece of theatre, thought Rose as she began researching the various card hands. Spades and hearts, what would Ruth Rendell or Agatha Christie have made of that in their murder plots. The boy who had fallen on the steps was not in costume, but the woman had been. Rose now realised it was the same as the card. She was dressed as the Queen of Hearts.

Rose looked up both performers' profiles on the Fringe site. They were similar in age, early twenties, but from what she could see that was about all they had in common. One was an independent performer doing card tricks, the other was a young journalist and performer who had studied at Bath. The show she was playing in was a parody, called Alice Through the Fringe. Alice was being played by a woman called Lucy Gabler.

Mondays was the day Rose shopped for ingredients, did the paperwork and gave both Trixie and Rob time off. According to the schedule Alice Through the Fringe was supposed to be playing at 2pm. But even though today's performance was unlikely, the other players might be at the venue, packing up, or thinking of a way around the loss of a cast member. They would have spent money coming here, they might still need to perform. But when Rose arrived at the venue, only Will Colby, the writer/director of the play, was there.

"It's too bad, a nightmare. This was supposed to be my golden ticket."

"What do you mean?" asked Rose. The director was thin, late thirties with long lank hair, tied back into a ponytail. He was sitting in one of the makeshift dressing rooms when Rose found him. There were costumes everywhere and props for Tweedle Dum and Tweedle Dee, the Mad Hatter and a huge red teapot made from cardboard, covered in crêpe paper. The props took up most of the limited space.

"I had TV people coming, I'd pitched them the alternative Alice a while back."

"So, are you going to be able to do anything?"

He shrugged, "It's too late to re-cast for this year now. Josie, she was the star. And now Lucy, who was playing Alice, has fallen apart. She's planning to leave as soon as the police say it's ok for her to go home."

"Where's home?"

"Cambridge, I think."

"Cambridge? Is she a student?

"Oh goodness, I don't think so and I may have got that wrong - Cambridge I mean. One of my sponsors recommended her. So...-" He opened his hands. "I'd never even heard of her before."

Rose noted the change in emphasis as he spoke, about not knowing Lucy from before, pulling back from knowing she was from Cambridge. "Have you ever seen this man hanging around, or at one of the performances?"

Rose held out the flyer Chris had given her yesterday. It was a long shot, but worth asking.

"No, sorry. No idea who he is."

"Was the woman playing the Queen of Hearts, Josie, from Cambridge too?"

"No, I've known Josie for ages, she was at St Aidan's, near Leamington. Small University specialising in humanities and the creative arts. I was teaching there. She started off in performing arts, but she transferred and graduated from the journalism program."

"Right, thanks, I'm so sorry."

"And who are you exactly, why are you asking all these questions?"

"Oh, just trying to fit some things together. My assistant found the boy who died on the steps on Saturday night. Is there anyone else that Josie might have known in Edinburgh, someone that might know why she might have been killed?"

He looked at her quizzically, his eyes shifted from side to side, "I have no idea," he shrugged. Then he began moving back, physically distancing himself. "Well, I need to get on, see what I can salvage from this mess."

His tone indicated to Rose that he felt little about the victim, his words were self-centered. Surprising, since he said he had known her for a while. But then, she reflected, given the situation the death of Josie placed him in, he was an unlikely suspect.

"OK, thanks, well good luck with that."

Two of the other actors arrived just as Rose was leaving. She waited outside the dressing room to see what was said, if the director told them who she was or that she had been asking questions. She guessed they had all been interviewed by the police. But she heard nothing spoken, just the sound of stuff being moved around, which, in the circumstances, Rose thought was rather odd.

The local paper had a full account of what had happened, but they didn't reveal the name of the victim. According to the reporter she had been stabbed once and died instantly from the wound. Rose shook her head, to be that accurate, the killer must have been up close and personal with Josie. Why did Lucy say she hadn't seen anything, they had been walking together handing out flyers for the performance later that evening? Rose knew the area was well covered by CCTV so she assumed the police would be scanning the footage. She walked back to North Bridge and stood where she had found the playing card. The CCTV camera must have picked up something, it was pointing towards her. A stabbing. Was that a man's crime or could it be done by a woman? And what about the boy Devon? The police hadn't confirmed that that wasn't an accident yet, but Rose remained convinced that it couldn't be a coincidence. How had it been done and more importantly, why?

"Penny for them?" It was DCI Chatterton, he too had come to see the area again. "What are you doing here Rose?"

She opened her mouth to speak, but she knew she couldn't fool him. He knew her well and she was a terrible liar. "I found the playing card here yesterday, after Josie was killed."

"How do you know her name? It hasn't been released yet."

Rose flushed, "I went to ..., to talk to the cast this morning. But it was the director I talked to, no one else was there."

"Because they were with me. Honestly, Rose, please don't get involved. I thought you'd have had enough of murders since last time."

"Well, I guess spotting the playing card and Trixie finding that boy means I am involved. Any news on how he died yet?"

The DCI nodded. "Yes, but I can't say."

"So, it was murder then?"

"Rose. Stop, please, let me do my job."

"I'm not stopping you, but this is my town too. What happens here is as important to me as it is to you." Rose stuck her chin out defiantly. She didn't want to fall out with him, she had grown to like him, respect him even, since they first met. He often came into the shop for muffins. Sometimes he seemed lonely. Rose knew that feeling only too well.

"I know Rose, but we will sort this, the festival is too important to have this stain of murder. I don't want that to be what people remember. A stabbing here in broad daylight, on my watch, is not going to be left unsolved. You can be sure of that. One of my officers will be in touch just in case you can add anything to what you told them yesterday, Trixie too."

She wondered if she should tell him about her conversation with Chris at the bar yesterday. Did the police still want to know where he was? But the DCI's rebuff made her less inclined to be generous. Let them figure it out, she thought to herself as she walked away and had words with herself about priorities. The paperwork for the shop could wait, she was on top of it mostly, but baking supplies most definitely couldn't.

One of the things that was a benefit of moving to Corstorphine was the proximity of the cash and carry. She used the trailer to bring everything back to her flat and then onto the shop on Tuesday mornings. Rose decided to take the steps and walk-through Waverley station before getting the bus along Princes Street. There were tourist shops there that sold playing cards with different Edinburgh and Scottish backs on them.

Rose showed the photograph of the playing card to the various shop staff, but none of them recognised the picture or could tell her a supplier where a card like that might be purchased from. “It looks pretty special to me. Have you tried the magic shop in Old Town?” The manager of the last shop had taken time with the picture, studying it. “I'm a magician on the side, I work with different decks, and they have a good range. Do you know where it is?”

“Yes, yes I do thanks,” said Rose.

Chris was performing later that day, so Rose decided to go and see what his act was about. She would have time to go to the magic shop on her way to see Chris perform. His show was in a pub at the top of The Mound and the shop was just off Grassmarket.

The magic shop had no clues about the card either though. “If ye find out hen, let me know, it would be a grand deck tae keep in stock.”

“Thanks,” said Rose. Her disappointment was palpable as she made her way to The Mound, she wasn’t much in the mood for entertainment. But Chris was right about his performance. He really did bring historical characters to life, and the way he spoke, changed costume, and added touches from his prop bag kept her and the rest of the small audience engaged. He did a particularly good impression of Einstein - just after he'd escaped from Nazi Germany - having a conversation with his armed guard whilst he was hiding out in a wooden holiday hut in rural Norfolk.

"Nice to see you again, thanks for coming," he said as she waited for the rest of the audience to leave the tiny room at the back of the pub. "That's me finished for the day and tomorrow. I'm hoping to see some sights. Are you free to join me?"

"Afraid not, well tomorrow anyway, my shop will be open. Muffins on Morrison."

"Ah the famous Festival Muffin, you have a stand near The Scotsman."

"Yes, and Trixie, who you met on the steps works for me, she is running the stand, the festival muffin was her idea."

"The girl who found the boy?"

"Yes. Small world isn't it."

"Yes, indeed." He hesitated, as if he wanted to say something important, then changed his mind. "Good for Trixie, the muffins are delicious. Tonight though, why don't you join me for dinner?"

He was good looking in an unglamorous way, very different to Troy. He wasn't overly charming, yet his manners, the way he looked at her made her feel good about herself. The way Sarah had before their holiday disaster.

"Please, join me. After all, isn't Scotland famous for its warm welcome?"

Rose smiled, "Alright, thank you but I can't be too late. I've not done everything I should have today."

Over dinner Rose told him she had been trying to find out about the playing cards that had been found. She realised she was over talking things over, trying to probe what she thought she knew, when she let slip their suspicions about him. Seeing him at The Scotsman and wondering why he had moved hotels. Chris explained that staying overnight in the suite at The Belvedere had been his brother's idea.

"We don't meet that often. We have very different lifestyles and didn't grow up together. The Belvedere suits his need for privacy, he's rather a recluse."

"Not like you then, a performer."

"No, quite the opposite. In fact we only met a few years ago, he's actually a half-brother – we had the same mother. Mum didn't tell me though. I knew she was divorced, but she didn't talk about her life before she met my father. It was only after she died that Nigel reached out to me. He was only in town for one night, so it seemed easier to meet where he was staying."

The way he spoke seemed genuine enough. Rose wanted to believe him, but she couldn't help wondering why he hadn't given the police The Scotsman as his address.

"Some sleuth aren't I?" she muttered as he declared himself flattered to have been given a starring role in her envisaged machination. Rose cautioned herself remembering Babs and how she had been fooled.

"Show me the picture of the playing card again Rose, please." He studied it carefully and then pulled out his phone. "Have you heard of him?"

Rose looked at the images from a website Chris was showing her. It belonged to an artist, Callum Blackwater. According to his site and the reviews his avant-garde style was on trend. His style was not precisely the same images as the ones Rose and Trixie had seen on the cards, but the way he painted faces was very close. Very close indeed, thought Rose as she handed Chris back the phone.

"How do you know about him"

"He was at my university. St Aidan's."

Rose tensed up. "Josie, the woman who was stabbed was also at St Aidan's."

"How do you know that?" Chris said sharply.

"I talked to the director of the show, the writer/director, Will Colby. Do you know who he is, or heard of him before? He said he had taught at St Aidan's."

Chris coughed. "No, no, I don't think I know the name. But, even though it's quite a small University, honestly most of us don't know half of who is on campus, unless they are in our cohort of students, or they come to attention some other way like Callum Blackwater. His exhibition drew the attention of the media and he left university with a blank cheque from an angel investor. Everything that Callum exhibited was sold."

Rose pulled out her purse from her bag and put some money on the table, "I really need to go. I hope you enjoy sightseeing tomorrow."

"Have I said something to upset you Rose?"

"No." She stood up, "I'm ... Look sorry, but I really do have to go, those muffins won't bake themselves." Rose was trembling inside, the memory of Babs and Troy trying to kill her were gaining traction, overwhelming her, until she could barely breathe. Chris had wanted to say something and then stopped himself. Was Chris teaching at St Aidan's really just a coincidence? She ran out of the restaurant and didn't stop until she was as far away from the restaurant as possible. Why had she told him everything like that, trusted him? She took a breath, remembering her counsellor's advice. Would the past trauma of what Troy had done ever leave her? She wanted a drink badly, to purge her body but she knew the only way she was going to be able to deal with everything that she was feeling was by going home and locking herself in the bathroom. It was going to be a bumpy night. The DCI had been right, she needed to leave this well alone.

Chapter Four

For the next three days Rose put all thoughts of finding out more about what had happened to the two victims to one side and concentrated on her business. The boy's death had been declared suspicious, but the media hadn't picked up that there may be a connection to the performer who had been stabbed or reported anything about the playing cards. Perhaps the police were keeping information, about finding the cards with both victims, under wraps for now. Rose couldn't believe the cards weren't relevant, somehow.

There had also been some other unsettling business to occupy her mind. A group of Neo-Nazi protestors had thrown things at a group of gay street performers who were publicizing their show. Trixie had had trouble with a couple of them at the stand too - after they had made racist remarks to a customer Trixie had refused to serve them. They had threatened Trixie and promised to burn down the stand. The police had intervened quickly and as far as Rose knew the two young men had been dealt with. She just hoped they weren't still in Edinburgh.

The festival was busier than the year before. Rose knew she should have taken on another apprentice or one extra temporary staff to help her through. With Trixie out at the stall, and the shop mobbed for most of the day she was exhausted, and she still hadn't caught up with the panic attack and sleepless night from Monday. The stress was affecting her ability to function. So when the DCI turned up, and she was about to close, he received a less than warm welcome.

"What do you want?"

"Muffins Rose, just on my way home and passing through. Is everything alright? Sorry we couldn't do more about those thugs who harassed Trixie?"

"Oh, thanks and I am sorry for snapping. I've just been that busy, and I'm going to be here until God knows when tonight. I've not much left."

"Two of those will do me," he said pointing at the almost empty tray of oatmeal cranberry muffins. "Perfect pick me up and one for breakfast."

Rose smiled, "Want me to heat the pick me up?"

"No, it's fine. Got time for a sit down? You really do look shattered." He pointed towards the table at the window.

Rose nodded, washed her hands, and joined him. The late afternoon sun was bright and the metal sitooterie table reflected dappled patterns back inside where they sat. "Do you want a cup of tea? I definitely need one," she said, moving towards the back kitchen.

"Thanks Rose, if you're sure. A black builders would be great."

"So, busy days?" she asked him as she served him the steaming mug of tea.

"Yes, like you. The festival is growing so fast, which is great for the city, but it has a downside. Pickpockets, scallywags of all sorts, well you know, you've lived here long enough. But this right-wing lot? Their protests are taking up quite a bit of time to police."

Rose noted the DCI had left murderers out of his description. Did a murderer or murderers fall under the term scallywag?

"I feel badly, about how we spoke the other day, there's something I should probably have told you, about the man who helped Trixie when that boy died on the steps. We found him, well in fact he came forward."

"He did?"

"You look surprised. He is just an innocent passerby, like Trixie."

"When was that, when did he let you know where he was?"

"Oh, a day or so ago, maybe Tuesday."

"I should probably have told you ... I met him too and had dinner with him on Monday. There's something else, although he may have told you, it's a website for an artist. His art, the style is similar to the playing cards. Look." Rose pulled out her phone and showed the DCI the images Chris had shown her.

"Callum Blackwater, never heard of him."

"Chris said his exhibition, even before he left University, launched him straight away. Pretty rare. I was wondering if it was worth seeing if this artist might have created the playing cards?"

The DCI paused, stirring the lumps of sugar she had put on a saucer into his tea. "Rose, you know I can't tell you anything."

They sat in silence for a few minutes. It wasn't awkward but it wasn't companionable either. Rose decided to change the subject. "Fair enough. But you can tell me about you, DCI Chatterton. After all, you know pretty much everything there is to know about me."

He laughed. "I'm nowhere near as interesting as you Rose. But I'll accept the challenge. ... What do you want to know?"

She made a face, "Why you're not married when you look like you should be."

"And you think I'm not married because?"

"Well, you don't wear a ring for one thing and you seem, well sometimes you seem quite ..." She paused, if she said 'lonely' he might think she thought he was pathetic.

"Aloof?" He helped her.

"Could be."

"I was married, Rose, but she couldn't stand the life of being a police wife anymore, and she ran away. With the milkman actually."

"Oh my, what a cliché."

"Indeed. It was the reason, well partly why my career took a bit of a downturn, DCI to DI, but now thankfully, I'm back in the rank I'd earned. You asked me about that last time, remember?"

“I do. I was glad when you were made up, promoted or whatever they say in the police. But no new wife then?”

“No Rose, no new wife. Just a busy career. Although not too much longer. Couple of years, I’ll be retiring.”

“And doing what?”

“Gardening, golfing, I’m pretty predictable aren’t I.”

Rose smiled. “Children?”

“We weren’t blessed, Rose, and now I think I’ve told you enough. Thanks for the tea and the muffins. Here,” He pulled out his wallet.

“No, it’s fine today, those were going to be day old’s for tomorrow and, well the tea is always on the house, we don’t do drinks.”

“Thanks Rose.”

Trixie came in just as the DCI was leaving. “Hiya,” she called to him cheerfully, as if he was an old friend.

“See you later Trixie,” he replied.

“Sae, whit did he want?” Trixie turned on her heel to face Rose, she was wide eyed and questioning. Have they charged them bawbags frae the other day?”

“He didn’t say. He came by for muffins. We had a chat about ourselves over tea.”

“Cosy Rose. But nowt juicy about whit's been goin’ on.”

“No, he’s not allowed to say and, I’m not sure I want to know anything anyways. Curious though, he didn’t seem that interested in the website I showed him.”

“Whit website Rose?”

Rose pulled out her phone and showed Trixie. “Aww Rose, I see whit ya mean. The style, that deck o’ cards, it’s nae the same, but it’s awfy close, ye ken?”

"I do Trixie. I do."

"Sae?"

"So, what - I'm too busy Trixie and after what happened last time ... these horrible protests ... frankly I'm a bit scared to get involved. I mean, they said they'd burn down the stand. Who does that?"

"Ay Rose. As ah said bawbags. But it's nae like ye tae be feart." Trixie pointed to the pictures on the wall of the cafe, Rose in her RAF days, when she had dreams about being an astronaut, until her eyes let her down.

Rose looked at the photograph of her in uniform standing by the plane. How confident she had been back then. Trixie was right. Fear was not usually her second nature.

"Alright, I guess there's no harm in doing some research, perhaps finding out if the cards from the deck we've seen were created by him."

"There, she's back. Rose the brave." Trixie put up her hand for a high five.

"After the batters, come on, we've got a lot of making to do."

It was after eight by the time they had finished getting things ready for the next day and headed home to their respective flats. Rose clicked back onto Callum Blackwater's website. She debated whether to email or call the gallery in London that Callum worked from. It was too late to expect an answer, but she could leave a message.

"Hello."

Rose was silent as the voice on the other end of the call answered almost instantly.

"Hello, who's that?"

"Umm, oh hi, sorry I was expecting voicemail," Rose said. "Is that Callum Blackwater, or sorry, do you work with Callum?"

"This is Callum. I thought I had recognised the number, but I guess not. Why are you calling? If it's about the exhibition being cancelled, I'm sorry, out of my hands."

"No, umm, no it's about playing cards. Someone told me you had designed some special ones."

"What? How did you know? It doesn't matter. They were a one off and sold. A private commission."

"Right, have you done any others similar ones I mean?"

"No, only, only prototypes."

"Prototypes?"

"Yeah, I was fiddling around with different designs before I came up with the finished deck. Sorry, who are you? If you want playing cards designed, as I said before, it was a one off. I don't want to do it again."

"Can I send you a picture of a card I found in Edinburgh, I'm just wondering who made it, that's all." Rose attached the image of the card and pinged it to him via text.

"Yes, that's one of my prototypes. Where did you find it, you said you were in Edinburgh?"

"Yeah, it's a bit complicated. There are two cards, I only have a picture of this one though, the police have the other one, the Queen of Spades."

"Wait." Rose heard various sounds of someone moving about, shuffling through papers, unlocking, and pulling out metal drawers.

Then the line went quiet. Rose spoke into the phone a few times before she realised he had rung off. She pressed redial, but it went straight to voicemail. "Hi, look this is Rose again, sorry, but if you call me back, I can explain a bit more."

Rose stared at the phone, willing him to return the call, but her instincts told her he wouldn't. What had caused him to hang up?

That night Rose dreamed she was the Red Queen, she was running through a rose garden wielding an enormous paintbrush that turned into a dagger. Tweedle Dum and Tweedle Dee appeared, "off with her head" they said, stealing the Queen's line as they ran towards her. Suddenly all the roses in the garden started to dance round her, forming a tight line and preventing her escape. Tweedle Dum and Tweedle Dee grasped feather tipped darts which appeared from midair – and hurled them at her, one after the other. Each one landing with precision close to her heart until she fell and bled slowly to death.

Rose woke up in a sweat. Her short hair was wet, clinging to her head and her sheets were soaked. She took a few minutes to breathe in, calm herself down. The dream had been vivid, and even now, with her eyes open and awake she still saw the colours of that deep red dress and the dancing roses, spinning around her. It was four in the morning, too early to go to the shop, but too late to go back to sleep, and she doubted she even could.

She checked her phone to see if Callum Blackwater had called back or messaged her, but there was nothing. What had he said when she first spoke to him, something about an exhibition being cancelled? She checked online. She couldn't find anything about an upcoming exhibition or a cancelled exhibition. She was about to close the page when an article popped up, it was from a newspaper, a feature article about Callum Blackwater and his millionaire sponsor, Oliver Moorcroft, dumping him. Rose clicked through to the article. According to the reporter, Callum's backer had pulled out of future sponsorship due to financial pressures. He was downsizing his business interests in Europe and moving back to the USA. The article was dated back to last Saturday. The same day Trixie found the boy on The Scotsman Steps.

"Curiouser and curiouser," said Rose aloud and then kicked herself for the reference. But as she turned on the early news her words seemed even more apt as she listened, horrified, to the headlines. A musician playing at Underbelly had been found dead just after midnight. Rose gasped, Rob was playing at Underbelly! Rose grabbed her phone and pinged him a text.

Please call me.

According to the reporter the unnamed musician had been hit over the head. A playing card, described as an *artsy version of the Queen of Clubs*, had been found on his back. It was the first news report to mention anything about a playing card and the report did not reference or mention that cards had also been found on The Steps where Devon's death occurred, or near to Josie. Rose wondered whether DCI Chatterton would be annoyed that details about this latest playing card had been included.

"Three of a kind," muttered Rose.

Her phone rang, it was Rob. "Oh thank God," she said.

"Have you heard, I can't believe it, I was with them last night, but I left early so I'd be fit for work, I should have stayed."

"Slow down Rob, what are you talking about?"

"Ant has been murdered. He was with a band from down South, playing Underbelly. It was horrible Rose, I didn't see him, but Tod did, he just called me. Told me to listen to the news. He's been at the police station. He said he found Ant just laying by the bins at the back. Someone had ..." Rob broke down, choking on his words.

"I heard about the murder Rob, I was so scared it was you, they didn't say who it was. What can I do, you're obviously not alright, do you need the day off, or to talk?"

"I need to go with Tod, back to talk to the police again, he's a mess. He and Ant were extremely close, and Rose, Tod told me that Ant was Josie's boyfriend, the woman who was stabbed on Sunday. What the hell is going on?"

Rose shook her head, trying to take in what Rob had just told her. Ant was Josie's boyfriend! Three deaths in under a week. Was there a serial killer on the loose at The Fringe? What other explanation could there be, and the playing cards. Was this a horrible and lethal game? A game of murder?

"OK Rob, well let me know how it goes with the police. I'm guessing our friend the DCI will be talking to Tod. I'm going over to the shop now, we'll manage, just do what you need to do."

"Thanks. I'll be over this afternoon Rose, but what about the orders for delivery this morning?"

"Don't bother yourself about it, what's happened is more important for you right now. Be with your friend. I'll figure it out, the local ones will be able to collect, and I can book a taxi to round trip the others."

"I'm sorry, you'll make a loss."

"Rob, just take care of yourself and Tod. Is he ..., well, I don't want to assume but are you and he an item?"

"Yeah, sort of, we just clicked, you know. He was the date I told you about on Sunday. He wanted to party last night though, which is why I wasn't with him."

"Well, if anyone knows how to offer solace at a time like this Rob it's you. He's lucky to have you supporting him."

"Thanks Rose. I'll see you later."

Rose dressed quickly and hurried over to the shop on the bike. Friday was a busy delivery day, she would have her work cut out calling the local cafes to pick up, but there was no way she could bake, deliver, and open at the same time. She phoned Trixie.

"Hey Trixie, any chance you could come in now?? There's a problem and Rob can't make it until later. I don't want to tell you why over the phone. Have you listened to the news?"

"Nae, not even put on ma' tunes yet, ah cannae be listening to the world's rubbish until later. Nae bother Rose, ah'm up anyways, ah' will come straight o'er."

Rose got to work on the baking. When Trixie arrived and Rose told her what had happened, why Rob wasn't coming in, Trixie broke down. The memory of what had happened to her two years earlier after she was attacked by Babs took her apart. "Och ah cannae believe it, Rose, this city, the festival, it's tae horrible. I just want tae goo, but I know I cannae, wi the stall."

"Trixie, there's no way I would expect you to open up the stall today. It's alright. You know I think I should just close. Start afresh tomorrow after we have shipped the deliveries."

"Nae Rose, we cannae, ye cannae afford it."

"Like I told Rob, it's OK. Both of you are in shock and to be honest I can't just leave it. I feel haunted by what's happened and I want to find out what these killings are really about. After what happened at the stall, and the protests, I can't help wondering if there isn't some faction here. Someone deliberately trying to ruin things for some sick agenda. The police have only said Devon's death was suspicious - I guess they had no choice but to announce Ant's as murder and there's been nothing more about Josie. I would have thought the CCTV would have given them a good lead."

"Dae ye mean yon horrible Nazi types?"

"Yes. But why would they pick on the Edinburgh Fringe?"

Och, did you nae hear, that whole area was oot on Sunday? Some sort o' power surge that knocked they cameras an' traffic lights off. It wis one of the reasons the ambulance had problems getting through. Ah was jist glad ah hadnae left onything in the fridge. It wis another stall holder whit told me."

"So, there was no CCTV operating when she was killed?"

"Apparently aye."

Rose bit her lip. “Right Trixie let’s get these in the oven and then we’ll call it a day. I need time to think, see if I can make sense of anything ... whatever the DCI says. “

Despite Rose’s best efforts the deliveries were all late. She knew she had made the right decision to close. Trixie, trying to help, had messed up most of the baking she tried to do and three of the batches had burned.

It was gone 10am before the last box was loaded into the taxi. Rose made them both big mugs of tea, along with a plate of what was left from the last batch of burned baking.

“I think you should go home Trixie, try to relax, and treat yourself. Finding that boy and these other two deaths has brought everything back, too close to the surface. Rose still had pangs of guilt about what had happened to Trixie. She was just thankful, she and Rob had found her in time.

“Rose ... ah think ah need to leave. Go hame - back to Fife.”

Rose stared at her. “Really? Well of course, if that’s what you really want ...” she broke off, not sure what else to say. Trixie still didn’t have the best relationship with her family and the last time she had gone back hadn’t been a great success, she had fought bitterly with her mum over church related issues. Forgiveness it seemed was a one-way street, her mother still refused to acknowledge that the family and their church had played a significant role in what had happened to Trixie when she was a young teen. And, if Trixie left now, where did that leave Rose? Closing the shop for a day was doable, but any longer, that just wasn’t financially viable, especially if she was going to recoup the investment in the stall Trixie had persuaded her to do. Profits were up but, Rose was cautious where money was concerned, she knew how quickly what she had built up could evaporate. Rose took a breath, Muffins on Morrison was her business and she needed to be businesslike now.

"I'm sorry, I understand how upset you are and I don't want to be unkind, but this is Festival month. I need you Trixie. You're more than just someone who works here, you put energy, creativity and have made a big difference to the success we have achieved. Commitment was part of what we agreed, after you finished the apprenticeship and I employed you full time. Maybe if you are just at the stall, not here, it would be alright? But leaving immediately? That really isn't an option, not for the business. You would have to give proper notice and then quit, so I can train someone else."

Rose could feel her body shaking as she spoke. She didn't want to be harsh or unfair to Trixie, but she was sure this rash decision to quit suddenly wasn't what was best for Trixie.

The silence hovered between them. Trixie concentrated on her tea, averting her eyes each time she saw Rose try to catch her eye.

Rose reached her hand across the table and smiled warmly. She had become fonder of Trixie than almost anyone else in her life and Rose knew the relationship they had built was important to them both. If she had returned to Fife, it would be a disaster. Trixie had come so far in her recovery and managing the fallout after what had happened to her, but she was still vulnerable, especially where her mother was concerned. Trixie's mother's choice to blame the victim rather than the church and demand Trixie forgive them was unconscionable in Rose's opinion. She had never understood religion. Her own mother had been spiritual, rather than religious. And Rose had grown up with an eclectic belief in something greater than herself, but she had no idea what. Perhaps that's why AA worked for her, placing trust in a higher power, as she understood it. But she knew even that didn't work for everyone, including Trixie, because of the higher power connection.

"We made a right mess o' these this morning Rose, or rather ah did," Trixie said, grateful that Rose had broken the ice. "Och, ye're right Rose. Nae, ah dinnae really want tae go. Sorry ... ah just panicked."

Trixie's impish grin was broad as she bit into a muffin, "Ye could say we murdered them."

Rose sighed, relieved that her attempt at bridge building had worked. "Ha bloody ha," Rose said, "let's put that thought into the calendar for Halloween. Murder Muffins! And Trixie, I'm truly sorry if I sounded harsh."

Trixie pulled herself bolt upright and looked straight at Rose..

"It wis wa' ah needed. Ye're right. Running hame, back tae Fife, is nae the answer."

"Trixie, do you mind going over last Saturday again? What you saw? In case we realise you had noticed something that didn't seem important at the time? Are you up to doing that?"

“Ay, course ah am. Nae more palavar. Where should we start?"

"Top of The Scotsman Steps, what did you see?"

"Well when ah went across, two people, both lassies, were coming up. I didnae go straight doon. It was a braw evening and ah stopped to take a picture on ma’ phone. I had the two bags, an’ I put them down tae do that. There was someone behind me, going into the hotel, but I didnae see who, then I went onto the steps. Nae one was coming up, or followed behind me, I was halfway doon, when ah seen him laying on one of the steps.

"OK, stay with that picture for a minute, what else did you see, or hear?"

Trixie closed her eyes. "Just the back o' him. The bottle of vodka was two steps below ... his body was straight across, on the top step, just after the turn. He wasnae moving and he took up the width of the stair, so after I called out and he didnae answer ah had tae move in tae the wall tae go below him. Tae see if he was awright."

"Did he look like this?" Rose lay on the floor of the shop, one foot underneath her."

"He wasnae like that, ah mean his head wasnae turned and he didnae have his arms oot like that. They were by his side."

"Like this?"

Rose shuffled her position, pressing her head against the surface of the floor.

"Och, almost exactly. How did ye figure it oot?"

"How to fall safely is one of the courses from the RAF. From what you said, there is no way it was a trip over laces.

His hands would have been splayed, he would have tried to stop himself falling. And his feet. Were both shoes undone, or just one?"

"Jist the one."

Right. Even if it wasn't a trip, his feet wouldn't be nicely straight, and his body probably wouldn't just be on one step. I think he was placed there, I think whoever left him there left him there to die, or thought he was already dead."

"The police ha' already said it was suspicious though, didn't the DCI say that, after we had been at the station right enough."

"Their response is all very odd. Almost clandestine. When did you see Chris, the man in the cloak? How long was it before he came?"

"Well, it wis after the couple came, the ones who ah told ye aboot. They both looked terrified when they saw me and ah called out."

"Do you think they were tourists?"

"Ay, Caucasian though, I dinnae know where frae."

"Blonde, dark, what did you see? Do you think they were part of the protestors?"

"Rose, they just ran off, I cannae say."

"Think Trixie, take a moment to see them in your mind's eye."

Trixie closed her eyes. "Aww this is mad, I cannae do it the way ye want me tae. I know wha' ah seen, that's all. Why are they important?"

"In case they turn up later, on the day Josie was killed for example. Maybe they were in the crowd."

"Rose, I think ye need to stop, ah mean, I shouldnae have encouraged ye, let the police ..." She broke off to look up at the door, someone was tapping on the glass. "Well, talk o' the devil, de ye ken who it is?"

Rose looked up from the floor to see Chris outside, he started waving at her through the glass. "Is everything alright?" he shouted.

Rose got up and went over to the door. "Hello, yes, sorry, just some logistical problems today. What are you doing here?"

"I went to buy a muffin for my lunch from your stand, but it was closed, so I thought I'd take a walk over and get one from the shop."

"It's a bit oot of yer way," Trixie called from the table, her voice was sharp, unwelcoming.

"Trixie! Come in Chris, we have a few, how did you describe them, Trixie? Murdered offerings and a cup of tea if you'd like one?"

"Thanks Rose."

Trixie left the table and indicated for Chris to sit. His arrival had thrown her into a mood. She didn't trust him, and she didn't intend to leave him alone with Rose. "So, ah'll clean up oot back and then see ye the morra once yer visitor has finished. Is that ok Rose?"

"Yes, but don't worry about clearing up, I can manage. Take the rest of the day, do something nice for yourself. Back to business as usual in the morning."

Chris and Rose watched as Trixie made a show of getting herself ready to leave, clumping up and down between the kitchen and the front of the shop.

"Bye Trixie," Rose urged as she slid into the chair opposite Chris and handed him the best of the failed muffins and a mug of tea.

"Sorry, it was chaos here. We, well Trixie had a melt down and Rob, my delivery guy, needed to help a friend. We were both off our game today when it came to baking."

"Sorry to hear that, Rose. Was it anything to do with what happened last night? I heard on the news someone else has been killed. The report said something about a playing card, it sounded similar to the cards we talked about when we had dinner."

Rose nodded. "Yes, it was to do with that. Rob's boyfriend is a close friend of the man who was killed and, it turns out - Ant - that's the name of the dead man - was the boyfriend of Josie, the woman stabbed to death on Sunday." Rose ran her hands through her cropped hair and then covered her eyes, leaning forward on the table. She had spent the morning being strong but now, saying it aloud, she realised just how much the three deaths had got to her too. "Oh my God. Sorry, give me a minute," she said and went to the bathroom to recover herself. "Breathe woman, just breathe," she said to her face in the mirror. Chris was looking at the photographs of her in the RAF when she came out.

"Nice," he said. "You look very lovely in your uniform, you still are."

He moved closer towards her and for a moment Rose thought he was going to lean in to try to kiss her, but he stopped, his body was close, she wondered why she didn't mind. They lingered in the moment, before awkwardness crashed in on the intimacy and Rose took a step backwards.

"I'm so sorry," Chris held up his hands.

"Don't be, it's all good, just well timing."

"Chris nodded. "Yeah. You're right and I really am sorry."

Rose waved her hand across the air and shook her head. "Chris, you were going to say something the other night. I don't know what, but I got spooked. You seemed to know too much about the artist."

"All I know is what I told you."

"Right," said Rose. She wanted to believe him. And now she was confused by what she felt and trying to normalise whatever had passed between them. "Look I need to clear up here, in the back. Sorry." "Are you performing today?"

He looked at his watch. "Yes, in just under three hours, at 1.30pm. I'm not sure it'll be a big crowd given its lunchtime, but I'm also repeating the performance at four o'clock, so if you're free later, perhaps we could have dinner? My treat?"

"Can I let you know?"

"Sure Rose. Ping me a text, here's my number." He handed her a card and was gone before she could say anything other than goodbye. She looked at his profile walking away from her shop, wondering about the invitation to dinner and what she would decide to do about it.

She had just finished cleaning and prepping the batters for the next day when Rob arrived with Tod.

"You closed the shop?"

"Yeah, well long story, but how are you two? Tod, I'm so sorry about your friend."

"Thanks."

"What do the police think happened?" Tod looked across at Rob and shrugged.

"Sorry, look why don't I make you both something to drink. Then you can tell me about what you know - if you want to."

"Thanks Rose," Rob mouthed at her as he put his arms round Tod and guided him to the window table.

Rose delivered the teas and joined them. She looked across at Rob.

"Well Ant's death is definitely murder, but the police are being weird Rose. It's like they want to keep everything low key, not say what's going on. If that reporter hadn't been there, I'm not sure any details would have come out at all, especially that playing card."

"Probably because it's the festival and the last thing Edinburgh needs is bad publicity about violence on the streets. The Fringe has a reputation as a place to be safe and there's been all this other business. There was an article online about the amount of fascist and racist activity here. The reporter was speculating it is a rising tide due to refugees and the current political climate."

"Rose turned towards Rob's friend. "Tod, you found your friend, is that right?"

"Yeah."

"That must have been horrible. I'm so sorry. Were you alone?"

"As I've already told the police, I didn't kill him. Alright? Are you done?"

Rose held up her hands, "Tod, I didn't mean it like that."

Tod put up his hand, his body crumpled. "I know, sorry, I didn't mean to snap."

"You know that Trixie, who also works here, found the first boy who died. Then I was on North Bridge when Josie was killed and it was me who found the playing card, the Queen of Hearts. It sounds like it's from the same deck as the one you saw last night. Trixie saw a similar card as well. The Queen of Spades. The thing is when I spoke to the artist who created them, he said the cards weren't for sale, they were a prototype. And then he hung up and he's not picked up the phone since. When I asked you about being alone, I was really asking rather clumsily if you had seen anyone else."

"Wait. You spoke to Callum, when? I've been trying to reach him since I found Ant. I recognised the card as his artwork immediately." said Tod.

Rose was surprised by his answer. "It was last night. You know Callum?"

"Yeah, he was at St Aidan's, with me, Josie and Ant. We were friends until he became rich and famous, then he dropped all of us ... well, except for Ant. Callum recognised Ant had talent. He tried to help him actually - but his angel, the investor, was weird and didn't like Callum being friendly with Ant. It was an odd relationship."

"Did any of you know a boy called Devon? He's a couple of years younger than you, perhaps. Canadian."

Tod shook his head, "I didn't. Ant or Josie might have. Why?"

"He was the boy from The Steps, the one whose death has been reported as suspicious, not murder."

Rob frowned, "So all three victims have been found with one of these playing cards by this artist, Callum. What time was it when you spoke to him Rose?"

"It was late, I was expecting to leave a message. I've been texting him ever since I found out about Ant and the other playing card. But no reply. When did the journalist turn up, who did she work for?"

"She was already there, she was doing vox pops on her phone with anyone who would talk to her, audience, musicians. An American woman. She's quite old and weird looking. I don't remember her name. She had gone out the back for a smoke when I came through and saw the body. She hadn't noticed Ant until then, although I don't know how. She started taking pictures right away, before the police got there and called the story in. I guess it was a scoop for her - right place, right time. Her behaviour was pretty mercenary, it was obvious it wasn't an accident, the way he was lying, with the card in the middle of his back and the baseball bat."

"Was it the bat that was used to kill him? Whoever did it just left it there?"

"Yeah, I guess so, it was right next to him."

"OK, so Queen of clubs, the victim was hit over the head. Queen of Hearts, she was stabbed wearing a costume, possibly in the heart, but what has the Queen of Spades got to do with Devon and why choose The

Scotsman Steps?" Rose flicked through her phone, searching for information about the reopening of The Steps and the Edinburgh gallery that had commissioned the work, but she couldn't find anything that linked Callum Blackwater and the playing cards online. Rose checked the time. It was already almost one o'clock. "I'm going to go over to the gallery, see if I can talk to someone about which artists were included in street art and the exhibition last year."

"I need to talk to Callum," said Tod. "And as he's not answering his phone, I'm going to see him in person."

"In London?" said Rob.

"No, he has a bolt hole, not too far from here, Berwick upon Tweed. A cottage called Terpsichore that used to belong to his grandmother, she left it to him. She was also an artist and painted there. He hosted a couple of weekend parties at Terpsichore, when we were at St Aidan's. And his angel threw him one there, to celebrate his graduation."

"Why do you think he would be at the cottage?" Rose asked.

"I'm not sure he is, but as he isn't answering his phone ... I can't just sit around here and wait for the police, the cards have to mean something."

"I'll come with you," said Rob. "Rose, I promise I will be back for deliveries tomorrow."

"But your gig?" Tod reminded Rob.

"It's tomorrow night. It's ok."

"Alright, let me know if you find him. Let's all touch base later. I'm thinking I might have dinner with Chris, the fellow who helped Trixie on The Steps. How about we keep in touch by text?"

"But I thought you thought Chris was involved. Have I missed something? I'm confused," said Rob.

Rose shook her head, "No, I don't think he's involved, but I think he does know something. Maybe I can get him to tell me. See you later."

As Rob and Tod set off to catch a train to Berwick upon Tweed, Rose headed over to The City Arts Centre at the back of Waverley Station.

Chapter Five

The 1.20pm train from Haymarket to Berwick upon Tweed was crowded with festival visitors returning to London and the South. Rob and Tod sat either side of the aisle across from each other for the hour-long journey. The scenic east coast with the sun glinting off the water drew gasps of wonder and delight from the passengers unfamiliar with the journey. When the train pulled into the station Rob steadied himself as he and Tod made their way towards the door. He recognised the short greying blonde woman standing in the queue just ahead of them and turned back to Tod.

"Look over my shoulder, the woman with the rucksack, isn't that the journalist doing the vox pops from yesterday? When you found Ant last night?"

Tod took off his sunglasses and squinted over Rob's shoulder. "Yeah, it looks like her, she's pretty unique. That's weird."

"Should we follow her, or go to Callum's house - your call?"

Tod shook his head, “I don’t know, maybe it’s just a coincidence, but let’s follow her, then head to Callum’s place. Terpsichore is on the coast road, just past Scremerston, we’ll have to get a taxi, it’s pretty remote, right on the beach, but it’s not far by car.”

As they exited the station, they saw the journalist heading for the taxi rank. “Follow that cab please,” said Rob, reminded of the last time he had said those exact same words, he had been following Tony from Old Town out to Edinburgh airport. Two years had passed since Bakti had been murdered and now here he was, with Tod, once again trying to figure out a game of murder. Why had he thought of those words, it was hardly a game. The last two attacks had been vicious. The taxi headed south.

“We’re heading towards Scremerston,” said Tod as the taxi continued along the A road, away from the town centre. Ten minutes later the taxi the journalist was in stopped at the end of a gated driveway. The gate was locked and the sign on the gate said Terpsichore. Private Drive. “Drive on,” Tod urged the driver, “until you get to the next bend.”

“What the devil is she doing here?” said Rob, pulling out cash to pay the driver, who was following Tod’s instructions. He pulled into a layby about a half a mile further along, out of sight of the other taxi. “Do you have a card mate, in case we need a ride back?”

“I can wait if you like.”

“No, it’s alright, not sure how long we’ll be, thanks though and, if it's ok, maybe don’t mention to anyone where you dropped us.”

The driver tapped his nose and nodded.

It was about a fifteen-minute walk back to the house. Tod pointed to a footpath that cut through to the beach behind where the driver had dropped them. "We can go that way to the front of the house, rather than using the driveway. There's a path along the top."

They looked down from the footpath onto the beach. The soft yellow sand was packed with families and children eating ice creams, picnicking, and building sandcastles. Rob wished he and Tod were here for pleasure and could walk barefoot along the shoreline together.

"Nice place, I don't know why I haven't been here before."

"Yeah, it was perfect when Callum invited us up. No neighbours, beautiful sunsets, and pretty much anything went if you know what I mean."

Rob nodded. He knew Tod would have a past love life, but he didn't want to know about it. There was a ten-year gap between them, and Rob had been worried Tod would find him too old when they first met, but it wasn't age that had come between them being able to enjoy each other. If only it was that simple, he mused. "So, when did Callum inherit the cottage?"

"I dunno, he had it before we met, before he started at Uni. It was his Gran's money that made that possible. According to him he was her protégé. She had been a dancer, I guess that's why the cottage is called Terpsichore. She fell in love with a painter and became a painter herself when she was too old to dance. She was quite successful, locally at least. Callum was full of stories about her, Russian

Mafia, the CIA, spying against the Nazi's you name it, he had a story. He never talked about his grandfather, well I suppose he died when Callum was quite young. At least, I got the impression he didn't really know who he was."

"But were any of the stories true, do you think?"

"I don't know, Callum is, well ... he's odd. He can be charming and fun one minute, then brooding, disquieting the next and you don't see it coming. He and Josie, Ant's girlfriend, didn't get on. She said he was pretentious, after he sold everything in his university exhibition. Then Callum did something really mean. He said it was a prank, I don't know if he was trying to break Josie and Ant up, but it had the opposite effect. Ant and Callum didn't hang out much after that."

"What did he do?"

"It was during term time at university. Callum and Ant had been debating Israel and Palestine. Ant is Jewish and his family lives in Israel. He lost several family members to the war in concentration camps. Ant is a pacifist though, and he wants to broker deals that promote peace. Callum was pro-Palestine and very anti-Israel. The debate got out of hand. Two weeks after the argument Callum put GHB into Ant's drink. He paid a girl – another art student - to get made up like Eva Braun. Then he got her to strip the unconscious Ant and pose naked with him. Callum photographed them and then sent the photographs to Josie. Ant was furious when he saw them. He threatened to tell the Dean, but Callum eventually convinced him it was supposed to be a joke. "

"What about the girl, did Ant or Josie take her on?"

"No, the girl disappeared after that. She just left the university, presumably she realised what she'd done was not going to make her popular, and if any of the profs or staff had found out, both she and Callum would have been expelled. But for some reason Josie didn't take it that far. Then Josie changed courses, from performing arts to journalism, and really tried to befriend Callum. I think Ant begged her not to, but she kept saying he'd understand one day."

"Do you remember the girl's name, the one who posed?"

Tod wrinkled his nose, "No, sorry. I don't think she's important now though, do you?"

"Rose always sees connections to things that I don't. At least she did last time ..., Oh heck, I should text her and let her know about the journalist being here. What's the plan Tod, I can see the cottage?"

"What did you mean when you said last time?"

"The Morrison Street Murders. Rose helped solve them, I thought I told you about it."

Tod shook his head. "No, unbelievably you didn't. So that's why she was asking me those questions. Let's just knock and see if I was right and Callum is here, then hopefully we can ask Ms whatever her name is journalist why she's here."

"You don't think we should be a bit less obvious, I mean if Callum is here talking to her, listen in somehow?"

Tod pulled a face then nodded. "Ok, that might be smart."

Rob could see the building was in need of TLC, several slates were missing from the roof, the windows and exterior paint was peeling, and the once magnificent garden was overgrown. For a bolt hole, given the money that Callum was reported to have made, the cottage did not reflect wealth in any form. The journalist was still in the garden, knocking on the front door. They ducked down behind the wall at the side of the house, so that if she came down the path to the gate, she wouldn't see them.

"Come on Callum, I know you're in there. I need to talk to you about Olifer. I think you know what he is up to? Are you one of them too?" The journalist banged on the door again.

Rob looked at Tod. "Did she say Olifer?" he whispered.

Tod nodded, he thought he'd misheard and assumed she meant Oliver Moorcroft, Callum's angel investor. The reporter banged on the door and called out several more times. Her loud American accent contrasted with the comparative quiet of the cottage. Tod bobbed up to watch the journalist, when he heard her footsteps on the gravel footpath, She was walking back towards the driveway behind the cottage. She was making a call from her mobile, but, despite the volume, they couldn't clearly hear what she was saying.

"When she said, are you one of them, what do you think she meant?"

"No idea," said Tod.

"Sounds like she's left the property. I heard a car. Now what?"

"Let's go and find a way in, see if he was hiding from her, or if he's really not home." said Tod, standing up and stretching his muscles from the squat that hiding had necessitated.

"OK, but let's make sure she's gone, before we make too much noise," said Rob as he followed Tod's lead through the gate and up the path to the front door.

Tod put his head against one of the windows at the front of the cottage as Rob tapped on the front door. "Callum it's Tod, you here?" He tried both the front windows, but they were locked, and the blinds were pulled down.

Rob walked around the opposite side of the cottage to see if there was a way in. The double sash windows were firmly closed and locked on that side too.

"Kitchen window," said Tod, pointing to the west side of the house, "maybe we can get in that way." He led the way down the path that ran along the side of the house back to the driveway. The kitchen was at the back of the house. It had three latch style windows at the top of a large flat pane of glass. One of the smaller windows was open.

"No way either of us will fit through that," said Rob. "What about that side door? There's a porch covering it."

"Yeah, if we break in there, no one will see or hear us."

"Are you sure about this Tod, I mean what if he is there and we break in, he could call the police."

"He won't call the police on me."

It took Tod less than a minute to break the glass to the side of the door, reach in and open it. "Callum, where the hell are you?" But there was no sound or reply.

Rob and Tod went through every room on both floors, even up into the attic. There was no sign of Callum or that the cottage had been used recently. A thick pile of dust covered every surface, except in the kitchen. Whoever had stayed there last had done a good job of clearing up and clearing out the rubbish.

"I don't understand it, I was convinced he would have come here."

Rob shrugged, "Why were you so certain?"

"When things were going wrong, it was always where he came, even that journalist knew about this place, she seemed pretty sure he would be here too."

"True. Her questions were weird though. Well, there's no point in hanging around, I'll call that cab to come back and get us, unless you ... What is it?"

Tod was staring at the sofa in front of the window, backing on to the coast walk, overlooking the beach. There was a yellow silk scarf on one of the cushions.

"That scarf, I remember it from the photograph Callum took. The girl was wearing it like a dupatta, other than the scarf she was naked.

"Really?"

"Yes, and I am pretty sure he used it again, in one of the bigger paintings, he draped the model in it, she was lying on a towel on a beach, and again naked except for the scarf."

Could the scarf have been his gran's, it looks pretty old?"

Tod went over to the scarf, Rob was right, it was old, but very fine, expensive. The sort of scarf that, when worn, would make a dramatic statement about the wearer, as it had in the painting and the photograph."

"Look here Tod," Rob pointed to some papers with copies of sketches on the coffee table.

Tod picked up one of the papers. "These are very similar to the paintings he does.

"His gran's work or her husband's you think?"

Tod shook his head. "I don't think so. Look, this is one of his gran's pieces, it's quite different." Tod pointed to a large unframed canvas on the wall. It was of a woman in a blue dress carrying poppies.

"She was good, not that I know much about art."

"Let's just go Rob. Sorry, it's been a waste of time."

They taped a piece of card inside the window they had broken, Tod wrote a note for Callum, and they began to walk back down the drive to the main road where they had arranged to meet the taxi. There was a small outbuilding on the left. The chain and padlock that were fixed to the door had been broken. "It's probably nothing," said Tod, "I mean the place is run down, but let's take a quick look."

"Callum," Tod called out as he approached and pushed on the door to open it. The outbuilding was full, crammed with the usual detritus and garden equipment the building was intended to house. Neither of them noticed a single black stiletto, abandoned in the darkest corner.

.oOo.

Back in Edinburgh Rose had had no luck either. There was nothing that connected Callum to the exhibition or to The Scotsman Steps according to the manager of the gallery who was part of the commissioning process. She tried several other galleries but none of them had exhibited Callum's work or had contact with him. No-one knew anything about playing cards or had commissioned a deck of cards for a client. She texted Rob.

Nothing here to report. Anything happening at your end, did you speak to Callum?

No, Callum wasn't at the cottage. Wasted trip. We're going to freshen up, then have dinner. See you tomorrow, unless you want to join us for a bite.

Rose sighed. She would have liked to have joined them, but she had already sent Chris a text, accepting his invitation to dinner. At the very least she would have some company for the evening and she could do with that. It was past five, he would be just finishing his performance. She went home to shower. She was hot and sweaty after the early start and tramping about all afternoon, but she began to wonder if she would be staying home after all. It was half past six by the time Chris returned her text.

Sorry, friends from London arrived. Can you meet me at The Skandi, in Leith, I made a reservation for eight pm.

Rose knew the Danish styled restaurant bar, close to the beach. She was surprised he had managed to book a table at the last minute, they were usually mobbed, or had he known all along she would join him and booked the table earlier? She felt an unfamiliar tingling in her stomach at the thought of seeing him again. She looked in her closet, her clothing was utilitarian. She had rid herself long ago of the extremely provocative feminine clothes Troy had insisted she wore, and she had donated the green silk shift Sarah had bought for her last Christmas. Surely not everything she owned was black, blue, white or grey, she thought as she pulled out the contents of her wardrobe and drawers. But her search for colour was fruitless. She settled on white jeans, a navy-blue top and the white gold pendant necklace that had belonged to her mother.

"You look lovely," Chris said as he greeted her. He was waiting outside by the door and leaned in to hug her, giving her a kiss on each side of her cheek. The continental greeting wasn't a sexual gesture, but the electricity she felt at his closeness managed to throw her off kilter.

Rose smiled and shrugged awkwardly at his compliment, "Thanks."

"Busy day?"

"It was alright, Tod and Rob went to see if they could find that artist you showed me, it's a small world isn't it. Tod, Rob's new partner knew Callum too. I'd never heard of Callum Blackwater before, now it seems his name is constantly mentioned." Rose looked out of the window as she spoke, shifting her gaze onto Chris's face to see if there was any response to what she had said. But his expression remained neutral. "How were your friends from England, was that a surprise?"

"Yes, sort of, they're fine, just one night here and then off to Glasgow. A conference about coin collecting."

"Known them long?"

"Yes ... but enough about me Rose, tell me about you, fill in the blanks for me, why did you really leave the RAF?"

Rose's stomach churned. She didn't want to talk about Tod, or prison or how come she had started baking. So instead she guided their conversation to his plans for the rest of the week, before he went South, back to Leamington.. Every time he tried to ask her a question she sidestepped it, turning the focus back to him.

As the server brought over coffee and cleared away the remains of the dessert they had shared, Chris leaned in, placed his hands over hers and asked "Rose, what is the matter?"

"Nothing, it's been really nice having dinner out for a change." She looked down, flushing.

"It's been really nice? Rose, what does that mean? Why won't you talk to me? That first time we had dinner, you were so, well so open. Then you left, but then when I came to the shop ... I felt something, I thought you did too."

"Oh you mean when I blethered on, about solving murders and mysteries."

"Not just that. Look Rose, cards on the table, I like you, I really like you. I haven't felt this way about any woman for a very long time. If I am wasting my time, if there's somebody else, please tell me."

Rose fiddled with the pendant. "No, I don't have anyone in my life, but Chris, to be honest, I don't know whether I even can. My love life has been, well let's just say a disaster so far, and I'm not sure ..." Her words trailed off, she didn't know what she wasn't sure of. She had been abused by Troy and loved by Sarah. But in the end Sarah, like Troy, had wanted to control her, it was the reason Rose had ended the relationship."

"It's ok Rose, disasters of the past are what gives us hope for the future."

Rose laughed, "Did you make that up? It's ... well it's quite a cheesy line for an academic professor."

Chris laughed, "Oh we academics are flesh and blood romantics too, not just old books and dry dust."

And suddenly Rose wanted to be with him, to have him hold her. She told him that with her eyes. He paid the bill, and they went back to his hotel suite. They sat comfortably in each others arms until she told him she didn't want to go home. After he had loved her and went to shower Rose lay on the bed in the unfamiliar comfortable hotel room. She was the most relaxed she had been in years, almost in a dream state. She leaned over to see what he was reading, it was a hardcover of Dante's Trilogy. Dante was one of the characters Chris performed. As she turned the first few pages, she noticed some of the words were underlined. She was about to put the book back when she saw an envelope and a scrap of torn paper sticking out from between the pages, like a marker. The scrap of paper contained just one word. Terpsichore. The envelope was addressed to Mr D Yeo, in Canada. Rose's body jerked. She quickly closed the book as Chris returned from his shower.

"Have you read it?" he asked, watching her put the book back on the table.

"No, no I haven't. And now, I need to go, there are batters to be made." She hoped that the lie didn't show on her face. "Thank you for dinner Chris," She mumbled as she pulled the top over her head and stuffed her bra into her bag.

"Is everything alright Rose? Here, let me help." He picked up her panties and trousers from the floor and passed them to her. Rose bit her lip, as she struggled into the rest of her clothes as quickly as she could. She felt like she was going to explode with the inner turmoil and confusion that had abruptly turned her dream state into a nightmare. He must have seen her read the slip of paper, was there some innocent explanation why he had written that particular word on it? Why hadn't he said anything when she told him about Rob and Tod going there earlier that day? Her thoughts raced as she finished dressing. She walked over to the door, he followed her with his arms out and she knew she couldn't avoid the embrace he was about to give her.

"I wish you'd stay," he said as she wriggled out of his arms, without responding to his kiss. She needed to leave, without making him suspicious, but she couldn't do that, she couldn't kiss him ever again.

Rose took a taxi home and, without undressing climbed into bed. She pulled up the duvet and tucked herself in. She wanted to feel safe and forget the last few hours. She was also exhausted. She fell into a deep sleep until her alarm, set for 6am, jerked her awake. 'Missing Artist Callum Blackwater is wanted in connection with an Art Fraud that has wiped millions off collectors' investments', Rose heard as she switched on the radio.

"Missing artist?" she repeated. "When exactly did he go missing?" Rose checked her phone. She pressed the number she had used on Thursday night, the night she had spoken with Callum. The number was no longer in service. It was Saturday morning, less than 48 hours. Surely it usually took at least 48 hours before a privileged white man was presumed missing, and reported all over the headlines. But art fraud, well there was something different. Rose scanned the headlines on her phone hoping to read a more in-depth report about what Callum was supposed to have done.

The first headline was attributed to the journalist Alison Parks. The same writer Rob and Tod had seen at Berwick upon Tweed the day before. Alison appeared to have endless articles and references to the man who claimed he was unaware of the multiple paintings Callum Blackwater had sold, and further denied that his signature confirmed the provenance.

A small text in an online newsheet referred to a research paper by a journalism student, but when Rose tried the link it didn't work. An American paper said that businessman Oliver Moorcroft had been set up and that his move back to the USA was purely personal and nothing to do with the accusations of fraud. The article also claimed that Oliver Moorcroft stated he had been driven out of the UK by unscrupulous journalists spreading lies and rumours about him.

All of the newspaper stories carried the same photograph of a painting, of a naked woman wearing a bright yellow silk scarf, lying on a beach towel. It was called Aphrodite at the Beach and signed with the initials JWB. There were rumours that several copies of the same painting and other paintings were in the hands of multiple collectors worldwide. Collectors who prided themselves on their astute evaluation of art, who wouldn't come forward.

According to one art critic, all the paintings had the same model in them.,

Rose texted Rob and attached Alison Parks article.

Not sure if you have already seen this. See you at the shop. I have something to tell you about Terpsichore too.

Rob pinged back almost immediately.

I'll be there early.

Rose was relieved she had made the batters yesterday, it meant they could talk as well as get the deliveries ready. Rob arrived a few minutes after Rose.

"Where's Trixie?"

"She should be here by 8, I told her I was already prepped and not to rush.

Rob, did you find anything at all yesterday, anything that could link Chris to Callum's house?"

Rob frowned, "Chris the guy who helped Trixie, the one you spoke to?"

"Yeah."

"No, why?"

Rose flushed, she didn't want to reveal her amorous evening. "He has a book, inside there was a scrap of paper with the word 'Terpsichore' written on it. There was also an envelope, with a letter but I didn't have time to read it. The envelope was addressed to a Mr D Yeo, in Canada."

"Where did you see it, this book?"

"In his room."

"What were you doing in his room?"

"Never mind that, what do you think? He must have something to do with Callum disappearing, with ... With the murders?"

"Oh, heavens Rose, did you and he?" Rob paused as he saw Rose's face flush. She looked down.

"Sorry, none of my business. Callum wasn't at Terpsichore yesterday and the house was neglected, like no one had been there for ages, well except the kitchen. It was spotless, no rubbish or anything."

"What do you mean, about the kitchen?"

"Well, there was no food or any signs of anyone living there but everywhere else was dusty and smelled of that unlived in shut up smell. Everywhere except the kitchen. The counters were clean, and it smelled of lemon."

"What did you think, when you saw the kitchen I mean?"

Rob didn't say anything.

"Oh Rob, you've just realised that might be significant now, haven't you?"

"Yes, and sorry, I meant to text you yesterday about the journalist. That article you sent me reminded me. The journalist who found Ant was there too. She didn't see us, but she was banging on the door and yelling stuff about someone called Olifer.

"Olifer, you sure it wasn't Oliver?"

"Yes, we both heard her say Olifer. She seemed to definitely think Callum was going to be there. I'm not surprised that the story is already leading the news this morning, but from what she was yelling through the door, it seems Callum might be in her sights as suspicious, not a victim. And that scarf, the one that's in the painting the paper published, that was there on the sofa. There were copies of drawings similar to the painting signed by someone called JWB. Tod said the drawings were almost identical to some of Callum's art.

"Anything else?

"Well only what Tod told me, that Callum had taken a photograph of another student posing with Ant and that Ant had been drugged. Knew nothing about it."

What?"

"It was a prank. Weird right?"

"But Callum was definitely not there, he couldn't have been hiding?"

"No, we went everywhere, even up into the attic, which had been turned into a studio. It only has ladder access, but it's got everything an artist would need except running water. It looks like he used a hose from the bathroom for that, there was one coiled up at the bottom of the ladder anyways."

"And were there any paintings?"

"No. Just brushes and palettes and blank canvases, some already stretched, some were still just rolled."

"So apart from a spotlessly clean kitchen in an otherwise dirty house, the scarf, copies of drawings and a studio without any sign of paintings you found nothing. Really Rob?"

"Sorry Rose, I did say to Tod that you always saw connections with things that I didn't."

"I think I want to see for myself, Trixie should be at the stall today, but I'll ask her to close early there and take over here. Then I can go to the cottage this afternoon. If I get the train just after 2 o'clock, I can be back in time to prep the batters for tomorrow. We were just planning to open the stall on Sunday and there's no deliveries. Can you come with me or are you playing tonight?"

Rob nodded. "Playing – well, supposed to be. But honestly Rose, my heart is not in it after what happened to Tod's friend. It gives me the chills just to think about being on the same stage where Ant played."

"Yes, of course, it's awful, but it's important to carry on Rob, for yourself. You're good, you know that, right? You wouldn't have got a gig at Underbelly if you didn't have a following. I'm sure Tod will say the same. What time are you on?"

"Nine, so I could come with you, and be back on time. Shall I ask Tod to come too?"

"No, let's just you and I go, is that ok?"

"Fine by me," said Rob as he started to pack the first deliveries into the trailer.

Trixie railed at Rose when she arrived and learnt of Rose's plan. "Och Rose, are ye sure ye shouldnae just tell the DCI about all this, let him away tae the cottage."

"No Trixie, I'll tell him once I've seen what's there if I think it could help. It's in England, a different jurisdiction altogether. He would have to contact the English local force and what do I tell them? A scarf, some copies of drawings and a clean kitchen are not likely to cause any concerns without context? And anyway, all this about Callum being missing is really just the media. The police haven't issued any statements, apart from wanting to speak to him in connection with the fraud."

"Sae that journalist Rob, how come she wis there then?" Trixie said as Rob came back to get the rest of the boxes.

"No idea. But she clearly knew something. But that's not the story she's written about. There was also a link referring to some research. Did you notice the name Rose?"

"No, I didn't I couldn't get the link to work. Do you think the journalist thinks Callum is connected to Ant and Josie being murdered, because of the playing cards? But I don't see how. He was in his London studio when I spoke to him."

"And Devon," said Trixie, "everyone keeps forgetting aboot him. Anyway, that's me, ah'm away to open up the stall. See ye there Rob. Dinnae be too long with the rest, ah hae only got about two dozen to get started wi'."

"See you Trixie. Good luck this morning," Rose busied herself with the shop display, it was already 8.30am.

The morning flew past as customers came and went. Rose was about to bake a fresh tray when Chris appeared.

"Hi, good morning Rose. I've been waiting for a moment to catch you alone. You're a popular and busy woman."

"Yes, the shop has been full-on since I opened. Are you wanting a muffin?"

He pulled a sad face, "Well, I was hoping for a kiss, or is that not available this morning. I couldn't sleep or stop thinking about you Rose. Can we meet again tonight? I'll finish my last performance by seven and then tomorrow the first show is at three. I hoped we could spend some more time together before I have to go back."

Rose busied herself with sorting out a tray of biscuits while she thought about her answer. “Sorry Chris, I have already promised Rob I’d help him out with something before his show and tomorrow, well it’s just the stall, but it’s my turn, Trixie did last Sunday.” She kept looking down at the biscuits, avoiding eye contact with him as she lied about the real reason why she didn’t want to meet him.

“I see. Well, perhaps tomorrow evening. I’ll be finished by 8 and you have Monday off, right?”

“Well not off exactly, it’s my grocery come paperwork day.”

“Of course it is. I’m not stupid Rose and far too old for games. If we were just a one-night fling, you can tell me, you don’t have to lie.” His jaw was clenched, she could see he was angry, despite the intimation that he was fine with a fling. “Text me if you find you have some free time, Rose. I’m in town until Friday.” The bell jangled as he left.

Rose looked after him striding up Morrison Street. Was his invitation a ruse? He had to have realised she had seen at least the envelope inside the book. She thought back to how Babs had deceived her with feigned illness that had almost cost Rose her life. She shuddered. Perhaps Trixie was right, she should leave things alone, pass on what Rob had told her to the DCI. She looked across at the photograph Chris and Trixie had commented on, of her in the RAF, straight back, proud in her uniform with the plane behind her and the group of other female officer pilots she had served with. “I am still that woman,” she said aloud, pointing at the photograph, to the surprise of the two tourists tripping through the door.

"Great picture," said one of the tourists, an American.

"Thanks, sorry I was having a moment. What can I get you?"

She served over a dozen more customers before Trixie arrived to relieve her for the afternoon.

"So, I'm off to the seaside again," Rob said. He didn't want to let Rose down, but he was struggling. He had spent the night talking to Tod about what had happened to Bakti, the student who was murdered. He knew thinking too deeply about the past would lead him down a rabbit hole that would end him if he wasn't careful.

"Are you alright? I can go by myself if you're not up to it," Rose looked at her friend, concerned. She could see something was up, she knew him all too well. They had been through a lot together, too much to be able to hide the demons when they were hanging about.

"Thanks. I'll be fine Rose, and I know how to get into the cottage, we had to break a window yesterday. It's covered up."

The Saturday train was even busier than yesterday. Despite the open windows the carriage was hot, stuffy and unpleasant - and Rose felt nauseous.

"Thank goodness that was only for an hour," she said as they alighted onto the platform. Rob still had the card for the taxi driver from yesterday and had called him to pick them up.

"You thinking of buying this place then?" he said to Rob as he dropped them off at the gate."

"No, well maybe, is it for sale then?"

"Yeah, my missus works at the estate agent where it's listed but she says there's been no interest and the owner won't sell to a developer. Doesn't want the place torn down. Mind you anyone could promise that and then pull it down couldn't they. I'd just take the money and run if it were me."

"Right," said Rob. "Do you happen to know how much it's going for?

"No, want me to text the missus?"

"Thanks, not now, but I'll bear it in mind. I'll call you when we are ready to go back to town. Alright?"

"Yeah, see you then, although I'm off by 5 today. Seeing my granddaughter."

"Well," said Rose, as the driver reversed and disappeared back up the A road. "That's interesting."

"Is it? How?"

"I don't know yet ... I just think it is."

"What's in there?" asked Rose as they passed the outbuilding.

"Nothing, just full of gardening stuff and spiders."

Rose looked at Rob and shook her head, "I want to see for myself."

"What the?" Rob exclaimed as they went inside. Nothing that had been there the day before was there now, it was completely empty.

"Can you remember anything about what was here??"

Rob closed his eyes, trying to visualize what he and Tod had seen. It had just seemed such a mess, they hadn't really taken it all in. "Sorry Rose."

"Look at this," Rose was pointing to the floor in the far corner. It was a different colour and cleaner than everywhere else, as if something had been standing there for a very long time before it was moved. There were scuff marks from the space towards the door and drag marks across the floor. Rose paced along the outside edge of the mark. "Twelve feet by six, Rob, did you see what was here?" she said as her eye caught the socket in the wall. "Could there have been a chest freezer here?"

"What?"

"Rob, did you see a chest freezer standing here?"

"No, well, maybe under all the stuff. I remember there was a tarp there, it had gardening stuff on it and by it, we didn't look underneath."

Rose raised her eyebrows. "Well let's go into the cottage, see if what you saw yesterday is still there."

"Oh my God, the note!"

"What note?"

"Tod left a note for Callum, explaining about the window, with his phone number on it," Rob started running towards the cottage.

Rose darted after him, to inside the porch covering the back door. "Is everything alright?" she called, catching her breath. He carefully pushed through the card Tod had taped over the window from the inside yesterday. Rob reached his hand through the jags of glass to undo the lock. The note was still on the small table at the back of the door, untouched.

Rob picked it up and waved it at Rose. "It's still here which probably means nobody has been inside since we were here."

"Oh heck. So, whoever cleared the outhouse is most likely coming back. We'd better be fast and on our guard."

Rob nodded. "What did you want to see first?"

"The drawings, then the kitchen. I'll look at the attic last, then we should go. Is there somewhere else we can ask the taxi to wait in case someone comes. I don't think we should use the driveway to go back."

"Yes, there's a layby with a path from the top of the beach, we can go back that way, it's about a fifteen minute walk."

"OK, can you call him, ask him to be there in an hour, that should be enough time. Show me where the scarf and drawings are."

The scarf and the drawings were both where Tod and Rob had left them the day before. Rose picked up the scarf and held it to her cheek, "It's an old Hermès."

"How do you know that?"

"My mother loved fine things, but of course she couldn't afford anything like this. She treated herself to a Vogue or Harpers Magazine, once a month. They were her luxury, she had to hide them from Dad though. They were our secret. Maybe that's why I always dressed down. I felt guilty about wasting money on frocks and fashionable clothes seeing Mum have to make-do and mend, scrape her pennies for something new and get a row for it. But this, it's beautiful."

"Take it Rose, why not, what use is it just lying there?"

"Rob, do you even remember why we're here?" Rose folded the scarf, it was large enough to wear as a wrap. She placed it next to her on the sofa and picked up the drawings from the coffee table. "Wow, these are different, but look, this one, isn't it similar to the painting that was in the paper?

"Yeah, you're right. According to Tod, Callum's work was very much like this."

Rose turned over the pages, the sketches all featured the same woman.

"I guess we have to leave them here, but let's photograph them, so we have a record of them, in case they go missing. Can you take photographs of the drawings on my phone while I go and look at the kitchen, then the attic. Then we should probably go. I'll be quick."

Rose was in the attic when she heard the sound of a vehicle coming up the driveway towards the cottage. She scooted down the ladder as fast as she could and back to where Rob was still taking photographs. "Rob, did you hear that?" she hissed. He was engrossed in what he was doing, oblivious to the sound of the engine. "Rob, we need to go now."

The front door to the house was next to the living room, they looked at each other wondering which door the unwelcome company would use. If they went to the side door where they had come in, they would definitely be seen.

"Quick, this way." Rose beckoned to Rob, taking a chance on the front door, but it was locked and without a key they were trapped inside. The only other rooms on that floor were the kitchen, a dining room and toilet. From what she had seen there was nowhere to hide upstairs. Rob gestured to Rose to follow him into the dining room. There was a large circular table in the centre of the room covered with a full-length cloth. It was a terrible hiding place, especially if the table was moved, or worse, used by whoever was coming in, but it would have to do. They just managed to crawl under the cloth out of sight when the front door opened.

"Someone's been here. That side door window was broken. I don't know why we didn't do this last night." The male voice was gruff, his accent had a trace of Welsh.

"Oh shut up, probably just kids. There's no one 'ere now."

The other voice was English - Essex, Rose thought.

"I'll set the gas. With any luck this place will just blow before anyone notices anything and calls the fire brigade. Come on, move."

Rose and Rob froze as they heard footsteps move closer to the table. "No gas in here, just the fireplace."

"All the bedrooms, kitchen and living room. We'll give it ten minutes then ignite the line from outside, through that kitchen window I left open."

"Are you sure that's long enough to work?"

"Yeah, we don't want to risk anyone smelling anything. There are too many walkers along the coast path."

"And the girl?"

"No way they'll identify her remains, they might not even find them."

"I don't like it. Or leaving all those coins behind. What a waste."

"Oh, for God's sake. It's what we've been paid to do, and I'm not crossing him. So, let's get on and do it."

"We might be ashes, if we don't get out of here," whispered Rose as she heard the footsteps retreat towards the side door.

The porch door slammed. Rob crawled out from under the cloth, keeping himself low he went over to the sash window, it would exit them on the opposite side of the building. Rob unlocked it, but hard as he pushed on the frame, there was no movement, the window had been painted shut.

"They are going to wait ten minutes, if we wait to precisely that and smash the window, we should make it, it'll take more than a minute for the gas to respond."

"Depends on what they are using. I can smell petrol and he mentioned a line." said Rob.

"Yeah, I heard, but it's our best chance. If we try to run before the fire and they see us, I have a feeling they wouldn't let us leave here intact."

"Feeling the same Rose, OK we'll do it your way. Eight minutes and counting."

Rob punched through the glass with the leg of a chair as soon as they heard a small rumble. A large flame and then smoke began pouring out from the back of the house as they jumped in turn through the broken window. Rose pulled out her phone to dial 999 as they made their way through the overgrown garden and over the fence onto the coast path. Breathless she told the operator where she was and to dispatch both fire brigade and police.

"I wish we knew what they were driving," said Rob as he directed oncoming walkers away from the house. A plume of black smoke was building over the cottage and they watched flames dancing in the window of the front living room before the windows exploded outwards, sending shards of glass into the garden. Rob looked at his watch. "That has to have been more than the gas to go up so quickly."

"Connecting petrol lines probably," said Rose, "we are just lucky they didn't put one in the dining room." They could hear the sound of sirens in the background, but the house was too far gone to be saved. Why did they have to burn it down?"

"They mentioned something about a girl, her remains remember."

Rose nodded. "Yes, and coins. I wonder who she is, or was and why they had been told to leave the coins behind?"

The fire brigade and police arrived quickly. Three uniformed police were moving the swelling crowd of onlookers further back on either side of the footpath.

"Who called this in?" one of the police shouted.

"Me," Rose put her hand up, "did you get them?"

"Get who?" the officer replied, pulling his notebook from his pocket.

"Two men, they set the fire ..." she looked at her watch "exactly seventeen minutes ago."

"And you know the precise time how? What do these men look like?"

Rose shrugged. "We didn't see them, we heard them, we were inside the house."

"This is your house? Your name?"

"No, it's not our house, it belongs to ..." Rose turned to Rob, "Tod is sure Callum owns the house, right?"

"Yes," said Rob. "Terpsichore, the house belongs to Callum Blackwater, the artist."

Chapter Six

Rob's phone rang. It was the taxi driver, in all the chaos Rob had forgotten they had booked him for a pickup. "Can you see the fire from where you are parked? Yeah, we're fine thanks, but not sure if the police ... Sorry, can you hang on for a sec?"

A plain clothes officer had arrived, she was talking to Rose and conferring with the uniformed officer they had given their details to earlier. Rose signaled to Rob that they were free to leave.

"... It's okay. We're coming now. We'll see you at the end of the driveway to the house. OK? Thanks."

Neither Rose or Rob spoke as they walked past the two firetrucks and police cars that filled the drive to the cottage and spilled out onto the A road where the taxi was waiting.

"I won't charge you for all the waiting time, since you two seem to have had more than a bit of an adventure, what happened?" Neither of them answered him immediately.

"Sorry. Look, we will pay you for the wait but it's all a bit too close to talk about it," said Rob, taking pity on the man as he caught his eye glancing back at them in the mirror, on their way back to the train station.

Rose lifted her chin and turned her face towards Rob "The police will follow up with us tomorrow. That woman, the plainclothes detective, knows DCI Chatterton, from when he worked in England. I told her about what those men had said about the remains of a girl, that it sounded like she was hidden somewhere and there were valuable coins. I'm not sure how much she believed about what I said. I think us knowing the DCI helped her make the decision to let us leave, but she was decidedly unfriendly to say the least. The fire brigade backed up what we said about how the fire was set, otherwise, I have a feeling, we would be spending quite a bit of time at the police station being interviewed."

"Well, I wish her good luck being able to figure out tyre marks of whatever vehicle those men drove, with that lot all in the driveway. But maybe there's CCTV somewhere that will help."

"Not along here mate," the taxi driver interjected. "Nothing until we're in the town."

"You didn't see anything, did you, when you were waiting for us?"

"I was parked in that layby, several cars passed me, but no I didn't take any notice."

The taxi dropped them at the station with fifteen minutes to spare before the next train. Rose went to the booking office and upgraded their tickets from standard to first class. "I need a drink," she said, their earlier roles reversed.

Rob nodded, "So do I, you knew that when you saw me at Haymarket, but it's going to be coffee, lots of it and strong. Like us, right? ... Right Rose?" Rob pulled her towards him and stared at her straight in the eye. He understood only too well what she was experiencing, that longing for a taste that wouldn't stop with just one and lead to an endless binge. It was his turn to support her, the way she had done earlier. Rob knew no-one except an addict in recovery would ever really get it. Tod hadn't understood, even though he'd tried.

"Will you still be able to play tonight?" asked Rose as they settled into the carriage with coffee and snacks.

"I will. You know, back there, when we were in that room and didn't know how we were going to get out, playing that gig – and both of us surviving - was all I could think about. When I smashed that chair into the window, I didn't think it was going to work, but I gave it everything. I don't think I have ever been more determined to live."

"I should have pressed 999 earlier, as soon as we heard what they were going to do, I was ... I wasn't thinking." The words that she was absolutely terrified, frozen, stuck in her throat.

"Rose, you were brilliant. And we did what we needed to do, if those men had heard us, I don't think we would be sitting here on the train going home, do you? And I have a confession to make." Rob opened his shoulder satchel and showed Rose the yellow fabric. "I didn't see the point in leaving it for whoever, when you loved it so much."

Rose shook her head in disbelief. "Well done Rob, but not because you thought I would like it, I think you just might have saved an important piece of evidence from going up in smoke."

"There is that. What do you think will happen now?"

"I'm going to call DCI Chatterton, before he hears about us from the English police, show him the photographs of the drawings you managed to take."

"I didn't have a chance to get all of them before those men came. I can't stop wondering why they had to burn it down. The place. I mean, there was nothing there."

"Well obviously not Callum for the insurance. But who else unless ..."

"What?"

"Well Callum is missing. And that kitchen, the fact that it was so clean, when everywhere else wasn't. Whoever paid them to torch the place must have been worried about evidence of some sort."

"Do you think Callum was killed there?"

Rose made a face. "Or killed someone there. The girl they mentioned? I don't know what to think about everything that's rumbling around in my head. I keep seeing connections, but then they evaporate. I need to write it all down, it will clear the fog."

"That's what you did last time, how you solved the puzzle. Lists and maps, they were all over the walls at one point."

"But I didn't solve it last time, did I? I had no idea Babs was ... and if you hadn't come along when you did."

"Rose, you would have been fine, by the time I got there, you were the one fighting back."

Rose looked out of the window, "Was I though?"

"You need to trust yourself, Rose. We both need to."

"I know Rob. I'll make a map when I get home. I am sure it will help."

"What about prepping the batters for tomorrow?"

"I have already texted Trixie. She's agreed to manage the prep tonight, then I can work the stall tomorrow. I really need to get my head clear. Not just about the murders." Rose looked down. She wanted to tell Rob about her eye. To explain it wasn't just what was happening that was pulling her down. But she didn't want to burden him after the day they'd already had, and because he was playing later. But if she was going to survive the night, she knew what she needed to do.

"Why don't you come to the gig?"

"Thanks Rob, I might just do that. What I said back at the station, thanks for holding onto me." The train was pulling into Edinburgh Parkway. "I'm going to get off here, it's quicker than going in and coming back out. I'll text. Good luck tonight Rob."

Rob watched her walk along the platform as the train shunted forward towards Edinburgh. He was worried, he wasn't convinced Rose was as strong as she had said. He phoned Trixie.

"What are your plans?"

"Och well nae date for me the night. It's ok, ah am just havin' a wee moan, dinnae tell Rose."

"Sorry Trixie. Look earlier, there was a fire, it's shaken us both up but there's something else on Rose's mind and I have to do the gig. I'm worried about her, could you make an excuse to call her later?"

"Ay, course, ah'm worried tae. I'll go round soon as ah finished prepping, that way she cannae lie." They both knew the desperate measures an addict would go to to hide a relapse.

.oOo.

Rose got off the tram and hesitated outside the local supermarket. She pulled out her phone, her gremlin had her in its grip, she knew Rob had seen it, in the same way she had known what was going on for him earlier. There was a recovery meeting in half an hour, if only she could hold on for that. Walking away from her flat towards the hall where the meeting was held, she reflected over the past months. Since the holiday and problems with her eye she had been running on empty. She hadn't reached out for help, taken the time to talk to her sponsor or a counsellor. The strained relationship with her Dad was bothering her too. He was old now, and alone. Despite knowing her conviction for fraud had been revoked and Troy and Babs were serving sentences for killing her mother, he still hadn't overcome his disappointment in his only daughter, accepting her as an independent spirit. Rose knew she should never have told him about Sarah, but Sarah had insisted their relationship should be open.

"Homophobia is not acceptable, Rose, we can't pussyfoot around the haters," she had said. And Sarah made no exceptions for Rose's father when he visited. It was then Rose glimpsed the similarity between Sarah and Troy. The subtle way of putting Rose's own thoughts and opinions down, making her feel she was always in the wrong, or worse. Rose knew Rob had seen it, he had questioned Sarah's put downs just before their holiday. And that had led to the rows which ended everything, after Sarah told Rose she had to choose. Ending the affair was not a choice between Rob or Sarah, or Sarah and her father, it was a choice to not be controlled ever again.

Her phone rang. It was DCI Chatterton.

"Rose, are you at home?"

"No, I will be later though. You've heard what happened? I was going to call you."

"Are you alright? Can you come and talk to me now? I will arrange a car to pick you up."

Rose hesitated, she wanted to talk to him, but she needed the meeting more. "Sorry, I need to do something, it's important, for me I mean. But later, wherever suits you best."

"Alright. In that case I'll come to you Rose, your new address. Around 8 will that be enough time?"

"Late night for you, sorry, but yes, that works. Thank you."

It was almost 6.30pm when Rose arrived at the meeting. She saw one or two familiar faces, but this wasn't her usual recovery hangout. Her sponsor was waiting for her, with another young woman.

"I'm glad you called Rose," her sponsor said, gently. Rose had once hoped she could step up and sponsor too, but every time she came close, she knew deep inside herself she wasn't there yet. It had been different when she had agreed to mentor Trixie, and other girls from the shelter - that was a work thing, and they had their own recovery support system. Rose hadn't planned to speak, but, in the end she shared everything that was happening for her personally, at length. Her feelings and emotions flooded out. The close call since she had got off the tram, the daily, almost hourly battle she had been going through just to breathe.

"Right now, it feels like having a drink would be easier, better, than taking one more breath without one," she finished.

She looked at the almost thirty pairs of eyes looking back at her, taking in what she had said, their acceptance of where she was, expressing encouragement to resist. To carry on breathing. And Rose knew that, for tonight at least, she would be alright.

Trixie was already standing outside her flat when Rose arrived in a taxi. She hadn't wanted to be late for the DCI and the meeting had run on.

"What are you doing here, aren't you meeting your new fancy?"

"Nae Rose, he can wait, are ye awight?"

"Did Rob send you?"

Trixie nodded. Rose was no good at lying and she was quick to catch others out when they did.

"Sorry, I know I have ruined your evening. I went to a meeting. Rob saw through me. I was in a mess. But I promise, I am alright now. The DCI is on his way over. Thank you for checking on me, and for taking over the prep for tomorrow. We all three seem to have had a moment this past week, don't we?"

"Ay, well at least ye didnae think o' going hame to yer Dad. You talked me oot of Fife and I'm glad o' that. Mind if ah stay?"

"No, of course not. You're welcome."

Trixie reached up and hugged her.

"Enough," Rose said, pulling away, "but thank you. When the DCI arrives, you and he can hear about everything that happened today together. Come on, I'll boil the kettle."

Trixie was speechless after listening to Rose tell the DCI about the fire.

"Well Rose you were right about one thing, we would have acted on the information you had about the cottage and passed it on, but I doubt anyone would have followed up that quickly. Are you sure you think it was a freezer that had been moved from the outbuilding?"

"Well, only as far as the size, height and shape of whatever was there, it was the switch on the wall that made me think of it."

"You say the men said '*remains*'? Is that right?"

"Yeah."

"They didn't say where?"

"No. But there was no one alive inside the cottage when we were there, I am positive of that."

"Well, nothing has been found yet. Please show me the photographs you took of the drawings. The DI you spoke to is suggesting we run a joint investigation, based on what you showed her. It's complicated because ours is a murder investigation, so her guvnor is taking some persuading that the crimes are linked. Callum Blackwater is now officially missing, in England anyway."

Rose knew the DCI wouldn't betray police confidences or disclose any lines in an open investigation, but there was something about his body language that suggested to her she had touched a nerve about the whereabouts of Callum Blackwater. Had the English police already been looking for him at Terpsichore? She opened her phone. DCI Chatterton opened the file he had brought with him and compared the drawings to the three playing cards.

"I don't get it. These images are totally different," he said.

"To the playing cards, yes, but look here, the style, like it's been copied. It's clearer in these tiny pencil drawings, look at the lines."

DCI Chatterton shook his head. "Whatever the DI saw in this, I don't get."

"The drawings are sketches for some of the paintings that Callum or his angel sold which has tipped the art world upside down. Callum told me the playing cards were prototypes he had done. That was on Thursday evening. No one has seen him since then. When I spoke to him, I assumed he was in London, but he could have been at Terpsichore."

The Inspector shrugged and looked back at the images. "Well, if Callum Blackwater is involved in the murders, he wouldn't have pointed the finger at himself by leaving the cards. Can you send the drawings to me? And you said something about a scarf?"

Rose pulled the scarf Rob had taken out of her bag. "This one, I think it's the same scarf that was used in one of the paintings, Aphrodite at the Beach. According to Rob's friend it was also used in a photograph Callum took of a girl with Ant - one of the other murder victims - when they were at uni together. The girl was made up to look like Eva Braun."

"Hitler's missus?"

"Yeah."

"Nice guy, this painter! If Ant was an enemy and he's now dead, it could explain why Callum's missing. But not why he would be dead too." He placed the scarf in a clear bag and labelled it.

"Because of the paintings? There's clearly a huge amount of money at stake, not to mention reputations."

The DCI drew himself up, he realised he was in danger of being drawn into a too familiar conversation with Rose, he liked her and admired the way she thought; she would have made a good detective. But her almost arrogant self-belief, in trying to solve things put her and his investigation at risk.

It was after the inspector left, and he issued his usual warnings not to meddle, Rose realised she hadn't told him about her meeting with Chris and the envelope and scrap of paper she had found in that book. She reached for her phone then, changing her mind about calling the DCI, Rose called Chris instead.

"Ah think ah should come wi' ye," said Trixie as she listened to Rose and Chris arrange to meet.

"I'll be fine, Trixie, I promise."

"Ay Rose. Och, ah just hae a feeling. But ah'm nae going tae row wi' ye. Ah'll see ye Tuesday."

Rose didn't admit to Trixie what she really thought about the man and the real reason she was meeting Chris was to try and photograph the scrap of paper and the letter from inside the book. Then she could forward them to DCI Chatterton. What was it Chris had changed his mind about saying when they first met, or again when he was in her shop?

She had arranged to meet Chris at 10 o'clock. The city was alive, still heaving with people and the heat from the day. Performers were starting late night shows and all the bars and cafes were packed. Despite her mission, the energy was uplifting. Rose was glad she had chosen breathing.

Chris was already at the venue, two hot chocolates in hand. He leaned in to kiss her cheek as he handed her the drink. "Is that alright Rose?"

"Yes, it's fine, why wouldn't it be? Thanks for this, it's perfect."

"So, are you all prepped for tomorrow, can I keep you out late?"

"Sure, well not too late, there is the stall, but I wasn't going to open much before noon. Sunday mornings can be pretty slow, one of the reasons I decided not to keep opening the shop while the stall was available."

"You're a good businesswoman I think."

"I try to be, I have big plans but something's holding me back."

"Like what?"

She stared up at him, conflicted. He was so easy to be with, what was his story? Rose didn't dare trust him. How did he know about Callum's house, had his appearance on the Scotsman Steps that night really been a coincidence? Was he the person who had passed behind Trixie when she took the photograph of the city? Was he waiting to see whosoever found the body? Why had he come over to the shop, was it to find Trixie, see what she'd said about what happened? The questions came at her like a swarm of bees.

"What is it Rose? You're frowning, as if you're trying to solve the problems of the world."

"No, sorry. My mind, it's not very restful. Not the world, just the murders here. I have so many questions ..." She paused, waiting to see if he would take the bait, tell her what he knew. But Chris remained silent as he put an arm gently over her shoulder and pulled her closer to him.

"Do you think we could take a break from walking?" Rose looked up at him, hoping he would suggest returning to his room, but he didn't. She'd have to make more of an effort. She put her head against his shoulder.

"How are your shows going, audiences alright?"

"Yes Rose, pretty happy, shall we sit here or are you too cold?"

"Well, a little cool, perhaps we could ..."

She studied his face carefully, she saw from his expression that he knew what she meant, but he shook his head. "No Rose, I'm sorry. I can't take that risk again. I don't play around you see and well, we live quite a distance from each other, I can see you have a lot going on. There's no space for me in your life. I'm right, aren't I."

Rose swallowed, "Well that's direct, I guess I am busy but, well isn't everyone, aren't you?"

"You have no idea how hard it is turning you down, Rose. When I came to your shop, the way you looked at me earlier, that was honest. I hoped that when you called me tonight that I would see the same woman who spent the night with me before she rushed off like Cinderella, but she didn't show up."

"Both hers are me," said Rose. "There's a lot you don't know. With me, in one way what you see is what you get, but my past, you know about the RAF but you don't know that I spent time in prison."

Chris gasped. "You Rose. How come?"

"My ex set me up for fraud, after he and his mother killed mine."

"It's all been sorted now, and they are serving time. So, what you're seeing Chris is someone with, what's the word, baggage. Such a cliché, but it's true." Rose hoped she had told him enough, but not too much, she didn't want him to pity or patronise her. But at this point she was willing to say just about anything to get her hands on the letter and that bit of paper.

The bells of St Giles rang, it was 11pm.

He put his arms around her, "I'm sorry Rose, I'm an idiot. Look, forget what I said, if you can. If you still want to spend more time together, could we go back to your flat? I'd love to see where you live."

Rose felt like a first-time student, negotiating a tango with a skilled teacher. She was thrown off balance by his suggestion.

"Honestly, my flat is a disaster, and it's getting late. How about this, I'll meet you after your show tomorrow, at your hotel, then you can come back to my place. I'll cook." It was a desperate effort, but it worked.

"And tonight?"

"I'd love to spend the night, if that's ok," she leaned up and gave him a kiss on the cheek.

As soon as he unlocked the door, Rose's eyes glanced over to the side of the bed. The book was still there. She placed her bag strategically by the door with her wrap. As soon as he went to the bathroom she would grab the paper, feign an emergency, and run. But before any of that happened Rob sent her a text.

Turn on the news.

"Do you mind if we look at the news? It's Rob, he said to watch something, maybe it's his band live, you never know." If something about Terpsichore was on the television, Chris might give himself away.

Chris nodded and turned on the TV, but whatever news item Rob had wanted her to see was over, they had moved on. Rose sent a text to Rob back.

What was it?

Remains of a body found at that house. A woman not identified though.

"Are you alright Rose? What was on the news?" Chris opened the mini bar and poured himself a drink. "Do you mind?"

"Nothing important, it's fine," she lied. She walked over to the window next to the bed. The book was behind her. Who on earth took Dante around with them for light reading, although he was one of the characters Chris played in his show, "Why Dante?" she said lightly, pointing to the book.

"Well, why not, he's interesting, complex, brilliant."

Rose picked up the copy of the book and opened the hard cover. The paper and the letter were gone. She flicked through some of the pages, to back up her feigned interest, hoping to see at least the paper.

"Is this what you are looking for?"

Chris held out the scrap of paper she had seen before.

Rose nodded. "So, you did see me?"

"No, actually, I didn't. This is my brother's book. I ... I borrowed it from him."

Rose was stunned by the brazen lie.

"You borrowed it? Really? And it just happened to have the name of a cottage that was burned down today inside, along with a letter addressed to someone in Canada, who was found dead. Who you found dead? The cottage owned by Callum Blackwater who's all over the news and might be connected to the murders here?"

"The book is my brother's." Chris clenched his jaw as he spoke. "Rose you aren't the only one with, what did you call it *baggage*. My life isn't straightforward either. At least, it used to be, but something has changed. Please don't ask me to tell you what. You may not believe me, but I had no idea of the significance until tonight when I heard about the fire. When we met, I knew you wanted me to bring you here. I could see that your head was spinning with questions. Your deception intrigued me, and I wondered how far you were prepared to go. I had no idea why. Then I remembered seeing you holding that book before you rushed off. I put two and two together, something about this paper meant something to you, so I fished it out of the wastepaper, just now in fact when I saw you pick up the book."

"And the letter?"

"Please don't ask me, Rose. I will give it to the police, but I need to do something first. I can't tell you what that is without risking putting you in danger."

Rose looked across the room, where Chris was sitting. There was a small wastepaper basket next to the desk. He could easily have picked it up without her seeing him while she was looking at the book, but the letter? Rose didn't buy what he had said about that at all.

"I can see from your face that you don't believe me. Like I saw through everything earlier. Pretending to want to be close. But Rose, what you're really doing is putting yourself in harm's way. You have no idea."

"Is that a threat?"

"No, not from me."

She walked over to the door and picked up her wrap and bag.

"Well then, it's probably better I just leave, and we forget all about it."

He stood up, but he didn't approach her. "All about what? The fact that we are attracted to each other, or that you think I am somehow involved in what happened to that boy, or maybe the other murders? Don't forget, Rose, I study character, people, not just what I see or read about, I study them deeply. But you haven't studied me or bothered to find out who I am; you have been the judge and jury, I am guilty of some crime, without trial or evidence according to you."

"That's not fair, you really want me to believe you will go to the police with something that could be vitally important, that you didn't know the connection between the word on that paper and Callum Blackwater?"

"Rose, I can't tell you what I know, or what I think I now know. But I promise you, I will talk to the police, as soon as possible."

Rose pulled out her phone to call DCI Chatterton.

"Who are you going to call?"

"The Police, I should have just told them about what I had seen."

Chris sat back down into the chair and picked up the drink. "Go ahead. I will be able to tell them, prove, I had nothing to do with the fire or anything else. And, from now on Rose, I don't want anything to do with you either. It will be safer for us both."

Rose's hand paused before pressing the call button, "Safer?"

Chris nodded.

"Fair enough, but if you really have nothing to hide, you have nothing to fear." She put the phone back into her pocket and opened the door. She looked back at him one last time. What was it that he wouldn't tell her?

He stood with his back to her, staring out of the window, refusing to watch her go. It was his parting words, as she closed the door, that made her shiver. “Rose, please be very careful.”

Chapter Seven

Rose spent the rest of the night on her computer. She had tried to go to bed but her mind wouldn't take a break. She needed to find out as much as she could about Professor Chris Foley and his brother. According to Wikipedia, Chris Foley had an independently wealthy half-brother, quite a few years older than him. Nigel Foley was a numismatist who sourced coins for other collectors as well as building his own collection. Rose paused reading about Nigel and opened a new tab to see if there was any connection between him and Callum Blackwater, but the coin collector did not appear to have collected art, or at least none created by Callum Blackwater. In an age where self-image was everything Nigel seemed camera shy, there were few pictures of him on social media at all. His interests, apart from coins and medals, appeared to be historical and ancient artefacts. Rose wondered how Chris could have recently borrowed the book from his brother when they lived in different parts of the world; it seemed unlikely that he would have brought that particular book with him to Edinburgh.

"Borrowing the book from his brother has to be a lie" she said miserably.

It was already 2am when she clicked on the television. The fire at Terpsichore was still leading the headlines because of a new find, a casket of rare coins found near the remains of the unidentified body. Rose knew the body was a woman from what she and Rob had overheard before the fire was set and wondered why the police were holding that information back. There were no updates on the deaths of Josie and Ant or Devon and nothing connecting the artist to the playing cards, or the drawings she had photographed.

Rose printed out the newspaper reprints of Aphrodite at the Beach and the limited information she had found out about Chris and Nigel. It was time to start the map. After three hours of cutting, pasting and moving things about, Rose spotted a connection. She sent a text to Rob.

Can you come over this morning? I have an idea.

Rob stared at the collaged map Rose had created. It covered her dining table.

"Do you see?" she said.

Rob shook his head. "Nope, you've lost me."

"Look, closely." Rose pointed to the image of the woman in the Aphrodite painting and the picture of the Queen of Hearts playing card. "He used the same model, I'm sure of it."

Rob studied the images and shrugged. "How does this help?"

"What if that's the girl whose remains they found at Terpsichore? Remember Tod told you about the girl who disappeared from university after the photographs? Maybe Callum used her as the model in the paintings? Then because she knew too much about the art fraud, Callum killed her at Terpsichore? Perhaps she threatened to expose him or blackmailed him. Somehow, Josie and Ant found out and he killed them too ... or had them killed."

"Whoa Rose, but why burn down the cottage? And what about that boy, Devon? And you really think, if Callum was the murderer, he would draw attention to himself using the playing cards he created?"

"OK, so I could be wrong about Callum, but what about the girl?"

"Yeah, I think that's a possibility."

"It would be better if we were sure." Rose drummed her fingers on the map. "There's something else too." Rose told Rob about Chris and what had happened at the hotel.

"So why didn't you call the DCI?"

"I don't know. Something he said that I had tried and judged him without evidence. He is really astute, the way he pieced together how and why I was behaving the way I was. I guess that's what he does to prepare for his shows, and why the characters, and how he portrays them, are so believable. Chris thinks I have called the police, perhaps he has called them himself by now. I'm sure that whatever he has to tell them will expose what's going on, if he's really not part of it all. Or maybe..."

"What Rose?"

She shrugged, "I don't know exactly. "He said he stayed at The Belvedere with his brother, before he moved to The Scotsman."

"You said his brother lived in New York."

"Yes, but Chris said he was here on a visit. Maybe he came over to see Chris performing. Wait, Chris mentioned a coin collectors conference in Glasgow that his friends were going to. His brother is a coin collector." Rose turned to her computer again.

"What are you doing?"

"Looking up that conference Chris mentioned. Yes, Rob look, in Glasgow, there was an exhibition and conference about coins and medals. Nigel Foley was one of the guest speakers. It was on all week."

Rose called the hotel where the conference had taken place. She pretended to have been a delegate who had lost her contacts book, trying to reach Mr Nigel Foley. But like the Belvedere the reception staff were well trained and unable to offer her any confidential information.

"Mind you," the young man on the end of the line lowered his voice, "many of the delegates were travelling to Chester for another coins and medals symposium. We booked suites at our sister hotel there. The symposium starts today."

"Thank you," said Rose, pumping a fist in the air. Then called the hotel in Chester. "Good afternoon, could you put me through to Mr Nigel Foley please." Rose ended the call as soon as he answered.

"Fancy a trip to Chester Rob?"

"Sorry, I can't. I'm playing two shows tomorrow and the evening one is our final gig. Rose, don't you think you should just let the police know what you've just found out. Let's be frank, both of us nearly relapsed yesterday. What about the shop? You can't just let it fail or not open the stand because you are distracted by this. You still have shopping and paperwork to do."

Rose stuck her chin out stubbornly. She had vowed after Troy not to be duped again and now she had allowed Chris to get close to her. Rose checked the time against the train timetable.

"If I leave now, I'll be there at 11.30pm, and back in time to do all the shop stuff tomorrow afternoon. The stall can close for one day."

Rob shook his head. "I wish you wouldn't go, Rose. What are you even hoping to find?"

"I don't know, but I know I need to meet Nigel, find out more about him. Don't worry, I'll be back tomorrow, I might even make your evening gig."

"Will you call the DCI before you go?"

"When I'm back, after I have met Nigel," Rose barely looked at him.

Rob ran his hands through his hair. He knew there was nothing he could say that would change her mind. "Well at least keep your phone on and charged. And for goodness sake text me."

Rose caught the train by the skin of her teeth. It was a long train journey, Haymarket to Preston, Preston to Liverpool and Liverpool to Chester. The hotel where Nigel Foley was staying was completely full and the prices were unbelievable. Rose managed to check into a cheap alternative, near the station. She planned to leave early the next morning and taxi to the hotel hosting the symposium and mingle as a guest at the conference breakfast. She hoped whoever was on the doors was not too vigilant.

The uncomfortable bed and lack of soundproofing meant another night without sleep. Rose was starting to second guess her rash decision to meet Nigel Foley. What was meeting him really going to achieve, she thought, as she made her way down to reception to check out.

"Everything alright Madam? Did you enjoy your stay?" the man at the desk inquired as she handed him her credit card.

Rose held her tongue from the actual truth.

"May I leave my bag here, I'll get it on the way back to the station, just after lunch?"

The hotel where the symposium was being held was a short taxi ride out of town. From the pictures Rose had seen, the location was stunning with views of the river. As the taxi made its way out of the main town Rose saw the streets were lined with flags and people of all ages dressed up in Roman uniforms and civilian dress in various styles, she supposed were meant to resemble peasant costumes of the time.

"What's going on?" she asked the driver.

"Oh, it's Roman week. Every five years, there's a procession, a feast, and a re-enactment of the battle. It brings all sorts of visitors. I thought that's why you were here. There was a huge find of Roman artefacts and coins here recently, so it's even busier than usual."

"Who found them?"

"Well, some say that they weren't really found at all. I won't say who, but rumour has it our town bigwig had stolen them, then pretended to find them."

"That sounds odd, surely there's a difference between finding an old hoard and something more recently hidden."

"Hmm, well some folk are too clever for their own good. Or at least they think they are. Looks like he's paying for it now though."

The taxi was about to turn into the driveway of the hotel when Rose asked the driver to stop and drop her by the gate. "It's a lovely morning, I'll just walk up."

"Right you are, love. That'll be £6."

Rose veered off the main driveway towards the back of the hotel. She peered through the windows into the dining room. It was well staffed. A gargantuan buffet breakfast was already on display, but none of the guests had come down yet. As she walked around the front of the building she noted there was a parking valet and concierge on the main doors. Inside she could see several reception staff, standing idly behind the walnut and glass desk, decorated with miniature roman shields. The gardens were immaculate. No wonder it costs a packet to stay here, thought Rose, realising that with so many watchful eyes her attempts to mingle with the registered guests might prove difficult. The concierge was already giving her odd looks as she pretended to take photographs of the rose garden.

"Lovely morning for a walk," she said cheerfully, hoping he wouldn't challenge her as she made her way towards the main door.

"Good morning Madam," the youngest member of the reception staff greeted Rose. The converted sixteenth century manor house had maintained the stature and grandeur of a house that must have once seemed formidable to the lower orders. Rose sensed a coolness in the greeting, as if her own suitability to enter the establishment had been assessed and found her wanting.

Rose walked over to the table marked Registration and spoke to the hostess. "Umm, hello, I'm here for the symposium," she smiled. "Not as a guest, I'm doing a piece for our local Roman History Society, in Bristol."

"Sorry, without a press pass or an invitation you won't be able to join any of the events."

"Oh, that's too bad, I've come all this way, I was told by one of the guests that it would be fine."

"Which guest would that be?"

Rose rummaged in her bag, playing for time, struggling to read the names of one of the afternoon speakers written on the events board. "Mr Martin Adams," she said finally.

"Mr Adams hasn't arrived yet. We are expecting him later on, he's a speaker."

"Right, well perhaps I could have a coffee or something, while I wait for him?"

The woman opened her mouth to reply when three of the lifts pinged announcing their arrival, they were full of guests. The hostess's attention was diverted when one of the women handed her an envelope, Rose slipped in behind the group and followed them into the dining room.

There was a short corridor furnished with two chairs, a coffee table, and a sofa en route to the dining room. Rose glanced into the dining room. There was no sign of Nigel Foley yet. She sat in one of the chairs, pretending to read one of the courtesy newspapers laid out on the coffee table. Facing the main entrance. The images she had seen of Nigel Foley weren't very clear, but she thought she had enough sense of what he looked like to recognise him. It was already 9am and the first event was scheduled for 9.45am. She didn't have to wait long, but it wasn't his appearance that made her raise her eyebrows - it was the woman walking next to him. The model featured in Callum Blackwater's Aphrodite painting. The model Rose had assumed was buried at Terpsichore. Rose let them pass, she wanted to speak to Nigel, but it was going to be harder while he was with her. If the girl whose remains had been found at Terpsichore wasn't the same girl who had modelled for Callum, who was she? And what was she doing here with Nigel?

Rose was about to get up and follow them when the woman came back along the corridor and went into the ladies toilet. Rose followed her.

"Enjoying the hotel?" Rose asked as they both peered into the mirrors and washed their hands. "Which floor are you on? I don't have a good view at all, it's very disappointing."

"Oh, sorry to hear that, we are in the penthouse, it's fabulous. We're hosting drinks later, before dinner, feel free to come, you're here for the conference right?"

Rose nodded.

"Nigel always enjoys an attractive fresh face, and I could use not being surrounded by old men who only want to talk about things over a thousand years old. Are you a collector? You're not the usual type."

"No, I'm not a collector and thanks for the invitation. That's very kind. Sorry, my name is Libby, Libby Parks. I'm a journalist." Rose lied, "You are?"

"Sam."

"Did I see you with Nigel Foley. Are you married to him?" Rose dared.

The woman laughed, "Oh no, getting Nigel to," she put her fingers in the air to suggest speech marks, *"put a ring on it,* is about as likely as getting him to part with his coin collection. See you later Libby."

Rose went back into the corridor and sent Rob a text.

Ask Tod if that student who modelled in the photograph for Callum was called Sam or Samantha and how old he thought she was.

The reception area and dining room were bustling; Rose slipped up the stairs, hoping no one noticed. But when she got to the mezzanine floor, other than an exterior fire escape, there was no access to the guest rooms higher up without a key pass. There was a staff lift next to the guest lifts, Rose took a chance, and pressed the button to call it. The young chambermaid looked puzzled as Rose stepped in. "I've stupidly lost the pass that works the main lifts and I'm late getting some things for my boss, Mr Foley. Can you pop me up to the penthouse, pretty please? He'll be furious if he doesn't get them before he finishes breakfast."

The girl nodded, "But you mustn't say I helped, please." Her broken English suggested Romania or another Eastern European country.

Rose put her fingers to her lips and said, "Of course, thank you so much."

Sam had been right, the views from the suite were spectacular. The rooms were lavish, no expense spared. Rose went into the bedroom and looked for the safe where she guessed passports and valuables, or papers would be. Usually, hotel safe codes were changed every time a guest checked in. No doubt Nigel would have kept the code secured, but Rose wasn't so sure about Sam. She went over to the unmade bed. A silk wrap suggested Sam slept on the left. Rose looked on the bedside table. "Voilà" she said aloud and turned the dial on the safe to correspond with the numbers written on the back of the wallet. She found two passports, two return tickets to New York, flying into Edinburgh and out of Heathrow, and a second ticket - New York return to Amsterdam for a Gerta Hoffman, a large wad of cash and a wooden box. She looked inside. The box was well crafted and held four pouches, each with four gold coins in them. The passports seemed genuine enough and so did the cash. Rose took a picture of everything including the box and the coins and then searched for anything else that might hold clues which would link Nigel to Terpsichore and Callum Blackwater. If Nigel had been staying at The Belvedere with Chris, where had Sam stayed? Why hadn't Chris mentioned her? And who was Gerta Hoffman. The ipad on the desk was locked and so was the black business case. Rose was about to give up when she saw a paper poking out from a file in the small vanity case under the chair. Rose opened the file, there was a receipt for a limousine from Glasgow to Berwick upon Tweed and some used intercontinental travel documents. A ferry from Harwich to Holland dated two weeks earlier. Rose photographed them, then checked the time, she didn't dare stay any longer. Either Sam or Nigel was likely to come back up to the suite before the first event. Rose opened the door of the suite and heard the purring of the lift already travelling upwards. She ran back inside the suite and with a minute to spare took the fire escape off the balcony, down the side of the hotel, back to the mezzanine floor.

The first person she saw as she entered from the balcony was Sam.

"Hello again Libby," said Sam. "Would you like to sit with me? Nigel is giving one of the introductory addresses. I'm only staying for that and then I'm going shopping."

Rose hesitated, she didn't want to draw attention to herself. She didn't have a delegate pass and there was a hostess checking names off as people went through to the auditorium. "Sorry, stupidly I've left my pass in my room, they won't let me through without it."

"Oh, for goodness sake, they won't dare refuse you if you're with me" said Sam and linked her arm through Rose's. Sam was right, no one stopped her as she confidently strode straight through, in front of the queue.

"Are you famous?" asked Rose, smiling as they found seats towards the front of the auditorium.

"Oh no," she giggled. "Not at all. But I guess because Nigel is so shy, hates having his picture taken, I've become quite well known at functions like this."

It hadn't been the answer Rose was expecting. Was she wrong, was this not the same woman in the paintings all the fuss was about? "Might I have seen you somewhere else though, your face is familiar," Rose probed.

Their conversation was interrupted as the guest speakers and officials came into the room and the other delegates began to clap. Rose's phone pinged, it was the reply text from Rob.

No, her name was Amy.

Rose held up her phone as if she was taking a picture of the podium and captured Sam's profile. She sent the photo to Rob.

Show Tod this, see if he recognises her.

"Nigel's on first" said Sam, "then I'm off. I guess you'll need to stay?"

"Yes, I really should," said Rose. "Sorry," Rose said and meant it. On the one hand Rose wished she could spend more time with Sam, find out more about Nigel and Chris and - if she was the model in the paintings - about Callum. But she was also desperate to speak to Nigel face to face.

Her phone pinged again.

No. Totally different, that girl was younger, with dark hair.

Rose chortled under her breath. Dark hair could be easily changed, but age? That was harder to pull off. Sam was still in her twenties. Nigel had to be at least mid-fifties, although he was looking good.

After Sam left, Rose had to sit through an hour of speeches and congratulatory remarks before the first break of the morning. She made her way to the side of the auditorium hoping to catch Nigel on his way through for coffee. She had no idea what she was going to say, but as it turned out she didn't have to, he came forward to greet her.

"Nigel Foley, have you made friends with Sam, I saw you two sitting together thick as thieves, do you know where she is?"

"She said she needed to go shopping, but she waited until after you spoke. My name's Libby," Rose said and put out her hand to meet his.

He had a limp grasp, Rose was surprised by the soft dampness of his palms when they shook hands. Rose sensed Nigel was very much a cold fish but did that make him a criminal or someone capable of cold blooded murder. They went to the coffee area together. Sam was right, Nigel clearly enjoyed a fresh face and more as she felt his hand wandering too close to her rear for comfort.

"Tell me," said Rose, "How did you find the show in Glasgow?"

"Were you in Glasgow? I don't remember seeing you there?"

Rose smiled, "Oh I thought most people who were there had come directly here, my err paper, couldn't afford for me to go to both."

"So, you're a journalist?"

"Not exactly, just a local interest paper in the Bristol area." The simple lie was growing arms and legs, but Rose realised the opportunity the disguise of a reporter gave her.

"It would be fabulous if you wouldn't mind answering a few questions for me. About your coin and medal collections and your other less well-known interests, art for example?"

"Art?"

"Oh, yes. I thought because Sam was the model for that artist, you know the one that's been in the news recently ... I assumed you were a fan?"

Nigel clenched his jaw and looked past Rose. "Excuse me, I forgot, I need to talk to the hotel about the drinks we're hosting later. Hope to see you there Libby." And with that he was gone. Rose watched him make his way towards the guest lifts and pull out his phone. He raised it up and, before she had a chance to move, she realised he had taken her photograph.

Rose shuddered and cursed herself under her breath. She had been clumsy, and now he had her photograph. If Nigel and Chris were in whatever this was together, Chris would tell him who she really was, and worse where she worked and lived. The warning voice of DCI Chatterton filled her head. "Don't follow the path of Icarus, Rose." Was that what she had just done? She texted Rob and attached the photograph of the ferry tickets and the receipt from the limousine.

On my way back. I may have put both feet in some doo doo. If you have time, can you find out who was in the car and where exactly they went in Berwick. Thanks.

Chapter Eight

It was almost midnight by the time Rose finished prepping, ready for Muffins on Morison to reopen the next day. She had been too late back from Chester to pick up supplies. Trixie let her know she was going to Rob's last gig. She had offered to help out before if Rose needed her, but Rose refused. Rose was feeling guilty, she had already piled extra work onto Trixie. Even so, she was finding it a challenge to refocus, get back to running the business. Her mind kept wandering back to meeting Sam in Chester and the way Nigel had behaved when she asked him about Sam being Callum's model.

Rob had sent a text earlier about the limousine.

Dropped the client, a woman, at a hotel in town and waited for her. Back in Glasgow by 6pm. Same day that Chris met Trixie on The Steps.

Good work Rob. I'm assuming it was Sam.

Yep. Driver is the owner of the company. He took a shine to her, which is why he drove, thinking he might be on a promise, but nothing doing. His description was not so subtle.

I get it, well she is a looker.

Chris was at the early gig. He didn't wait around to speak though.

Rose shivered when she read that. Why had Chris gone to Rob's gig, was he hoping Rose would be there? Had Nigel sent him the photograph? She decided to get a taxi back to her flat. It was extravagant after all the other expenses and closing the stall, but after two nights of not sleeping and knowing Chris might be looking for her, she didn't feel safe. Even if she went straight to bed, she'd only get about six hours before it was time to leave again. As she flicked on the hall light she was surprised to find a white envelope had been pushed under her door. All the post was delivered in the post basket in the main entrance of the tenement and whichever tenant was first down usually sorted it onto the table. Whoever had left this for her had been inside the building. There was nothing written on the envelope. She opened it carefully and took out a sheet of blank folded paper wrapped around a playing card. The Queen of Diamonds. The card was from a regular deck that looked like it could be bought anywhere. On the front of the card, over the face of the queen, someone had drawn a question mark in red permanent marker.

Rose put the card on the table next to the map, not wanting to touch it. She put the envelope next to it. Was this a threat, or a prompt to find out who the killer was? Despite her earlier concerns about Chris, she convinced herself it was the latter. Rose pulled out her phone, took a photograph, and sent the picture to Rob with a text.

Look what was pushed under my door.

Rose, tell the DCI straight away. Want me to come over?

No, I'm so shattered, but thanks. I'm going to sleep on it, wait until morning. I'm well locked up. It doesn't feel like a personal threat.

I'll be at the shop first thing Rose. Take care. I'm here if you change your mind.

Thanks, goodnight.

That night Rose dreamed she was carrying a torch and running down a never-ending circular staircase taking her deeper and deeper underground. Each time she thought she was at the bottom, a door opened to more steps. Some of the steps were narrow, others wide, they varied in height, and she slipped a few times, misjudging where to put her feet in the darkness. She finally landed on the bottom of the staircase and stepped onto the floor of a long passageway, covered in tiny red and black squares. There was a little table in the corner with a bottle - similar to the one in the Alice in Wonderland book she had had as a child - which said *Drink Me*. A knave stood outside each of the four doors on either side of the hallway, they were dressed in the uniform of the four card suits, Diamonds, Clubs, Spades and Hearts. They turned to face her.

Rose woke with a jolt as if her body had left and rejoined her. Had she been wrong about the playing card, was it a threat after all?

It was just before 6am when Rose reached for her phone, put on the radio for the news and set about making coffee. The headline sent chills down her spine, and she spilled the boiling water over her arm. "A third victim in a series of Murders at The Edinburgh Fringe Festival was discovered by tourists on a ghost walking tour. The unnamed victim is believed to be a professor who was also taking part in a series of performances at the Fringe Festival. A spokesperson from the police will be issuing a statement about the murders later this morning."

Rose ran cold water over the burn and sent Rob a text.

Another murder. I think the victim is Chris.

She held onto the phone, blaming herself for not calling the DCI last night. Could the card she had received been a warning about the next murder? And, if Chris was the victim, none of what she had seen or thought she had found out yesterday made any sense at all. But how many other professors were likely to have been performing at the festival? Rose went over to the table where she had left the playing card, paper and envelope. She stared at them, willing them to reveal how and who had delivered them and more importantly, why. Her call to DCI Chatterton went straight to voicemail.

"It's Rose McLaren. Sorry, I probably should have called last night, I just heard the news. Was there a card with the body, the Queen of Diamonds? Someone delivered that playing card to my house yesterday, I don't know when. Did you speak to Professor Foley about a letter? Is it ..." her voice broke off and she hung up. What was the point in asking the question? She knew the DCI wouldn't tell her who the victim was until the news was public. She phoned The Scotsman hotel and asked to be put through to Chris Foley's room.

"I'm sorry, who is this calling? No calls can be put through at the moment, but we have been asked to record all calls for the guest." The woman's voice was calm." It told her what she needed to know. The murdered man was Chris.

Rose hung up, dressed quickly and made her way to the shop.

"God Rose, what the heck." Rob said as he arrived at the shop, a few minutes after Rose.

Rose nodded and then shrugged. "I left a message for the DCI, I'm guessing he'll come here at some point, I let him know about the playing card. There was no mention of a playing card on the radio and the report said there had only been three murders."

"Well, reporters make mistakes all the time. If we assume that the murder last night is connected to the other three here in Edinburgh, and they all have the playing cards in common, what does that suggest? I hate to keep saying a game, but that's what it feels like, that someone, someone evil, is playing a game."

"I know," said Rose. "I thought that earlier. Yesterday I thought I had figured some of it out, but now, well I have no idea. Except we don't officially know that it's Chris who is dead."

"You do now," said a voice from behind. It was the DCI, Rob had forgotten to lock the front door to the shop and the DCI had let himself in. "What's all this about a playing card Rose?"

Rose pulled out her phone and showed the DCI the photograph she had taken. "It was on the mat in the hallway of my flat when I came home late last night. I'm guessing that you found an art card of the Queen of Diamonds with the body?"

The DCI didn't answer the question. Instead, he asked her, "Where were you yesterday Rose, which part of England?"

Rose swallowed, there was no point in pretending, she realised the DCI already knew where she had been. "Chester."

"And why did you go there, Rose?"

"Look, there's a lot I want to tell you, but it seems like you may already know some of it. I met Chris's brother Nigel and his partner, she's the model in the missing artist's paintings."

"Was going there a coincidence Rose, or did you go there to find him?"

"How did you know I was there?"

"You appear to have caught the eye of the English police, Rose. The DI wants to know more about you, why you were poking around the cottage that burned down in Berwick upon Tweed and what you were doing in Chester. They appear to have some sort of interest in Nigel and wondered when and why you had arranged to meet him. The DI you met in Berwick suggested you were er, now what was it she said? Ah, that's it, criminally stupid or criminally involved."

"Sarcasm doesn't suit you, Detective Chief Inspector," said Rose.

"Well Rose, why don't you tell me everything you know, everything that you should have told me before today and stop wasting everyone's time, or do I need to charge you with obstruction? How's that for sarcasm."

Rose was taken aback, why was he behaving like this? She thought they had a relationship based on respect. Yes, she realised she should have talked to him earlier but she wasn't going to roll over, take this attitude from him. DCI or not.

"I think you'll find that speaking to me like that breaks the code of conduct. Perhaps it would be better if my statement was taken by someone else, or at least witnessed by another officer."

"Oh, don't worry Rose, from now on any and all communication between you and I will only be done on a very formal basis. What time can you be at the station to give a statement?"

"Late afternoon, after we close if that's alright."

"I will see you then Rose. And make sure you bring that card and the envelope with you, in this. We're too stretched with all these neo nazi's for me to send a uniform to collect it." He handed her a plastic evidence bag. "Good morning."

"Close it, or you'll catch flies," Rose sniped at Rob who had his mouth open listening to the exchange of words. "We've got work to do here, but that little conflab has confirmed that the police are nowhere with this case."

"How do you figure that?"

"Well, why else was he being so sensitive? I mean, for all he knew I could have been legitimately in Chester, someone or something has stirred it up. But at least we know for sure that it was Chris who was found murdered." Rose's voice cracked as she said his name. Why hadn't he talked to her, trusted her?

"You OK Rose?"

"Yes," Rose wiped a tear from her cheek. "Now we just have to figure out who killed him. I feel responsible."

"Rose, Don't be ridiculous! He should have gone to the police with whatever it was he knew."

"Yes. But I'm sure that was what was behind the card at my flat, someone tipping me off, asking me to find out who the killer is. They must have known the police wouldn't reveal there was another art playing card found with the body."

"But we don't know that there was, I mean the DCI didn't say that."

"He didn't have to. He didn't exactly deny it, did he?"

Rob thought back to the conversation, Rose was right, she had questioned whether there was a playing card found with the body, and the DCI hadn't denied it.

"I wonder who identified his body? I mean, it's only 7.30am now, and according to the news the body was found just after 1am. That's extraordinarily fast given his brother was in Chester and any other family is likely way down south in England."

"How do you feel Rose, I mean given everything recently..."

"I'm good Rob. That meeting really helped me. Getting involved with Chris was me being stupid," Rose paused. Hoping her bluff fooled him. "But, the last time we spoke ... I feel bad that I assumed he was involved in the murders somehow. But, the letter he had, maybe he was? I still don't believe his explanation about how he had that paper with the name of Callum's cottage on it in that book."

.oOo.

The DCI hated to admit that Rose had been right about the way he had spoken to her. He was angry with her for getting involved. When the DI from Berwick had called and asked him about Rose, she had accused him of unprofessional bias. But that was typical of DI Donna Gibbs, he reflected. Donna had never been a woman's woman. She had been like that when they worked together in Lincoln. Donna had just been promoted and their guv had been a woman, very professional. But Donna did everything she could to undermine her. Reverse feminism, someone had called it after Donna's temporary suspension. In the course of his career DCI Chatterton had often seen male officers hating on women, but not women against women. It wasn't pretty and it had been Donna who lost out in the end. After the investigation Donna was demoted and transferred. He hadn't thought about her for years. He was glad she had eventually made DI, but he was surprised to find she hadn't married or was living with a partner. Donna was extremely attractive and had never been without a steady stream of admirers, or at least that was the way he remembered it. He had been one of them.

Since Donna had taken against Rose and both women had pulled him up short about his professionalism, retirement was looking more attractive by the day, but he didn't have time to think about that now, not with four murders to solve. The first death was still under review pending more toxicology reports. He would bet his hat that it was murder though. Rose was right, at least about the significance of the playing cards. He knew he should have acknowledged her help after she found the Queen of Hearts.

By the time Rose arrived at the station, DCI Chatterton felt more composed. The question over the cause of Devon's death was resolved, and his name added to the list of murder victims.

"I'm sorry about this morning Rose. I shouldn't have spoken to you like that." The DCI said as he handed her the watery tea.

"Me too," she said.

"So, what were you doing in Chester?"

Rose looked at the bag she had carefully put the playing card, envelope and paper into. "It makes no sense now. Before I went to Chester I thought Chris Foley, the man who was murdered last night, was involved in what was happening. I'd found a scrap of paper in a book with the word *Terpsichore* on it and a letter addressed to, well I think it was Devon. I only saw the envelope. Chris told me he had borrowed the book from his brother, Nigel Foley. What he said didn't really sound plausible, so I decided to check it out for myself. Chris told me he had something he needed to do before talking to you about the letter. Then when I arrived in Chester, I saw Nigel was with the model, the one in Callum's painting, except Nigel Foley denied that. He became quite weird after I asked him about it and I saw him take my photograph. I thought Callum's model was dead."

"Why?"

Rose shrugged. "I figured things out wrong it seems."

The DCI looked away and put his hands behind his head and sighed. "I have told you before, evidence is what matters Rose, police work is about evidence, not gut instincts."

"Yes, I know, but surely you have gut instincts sometimes, instincts that tell you when someone is lying, or when a lead isn't worth following."

"My work isn't like that, Rose, I have to be exact, test everything, even you. Everything you say, I can't simply take it at face value. I know you know that. When you were a pilot, did you ever get into a plane and take off without doing all the checks?"

Rose shook her head. "Of course not." It was a good reminder of process and procedure. "You're right and my instincts haven't been exactly reliable, have they? I mean, one minute I'm choosing to sleep with the man, the next I think he's a murderer, and now he too is dead."

"I thought ..." The DCI paused and stared at her. He was confused, uncertain how to respond to what she had just told him. It was none of his business who Rose chose to sleep with and he couldn't tell her the police too had had their suspicions about the man, although not as a potential murderer. The ticking of the clock seemed to grow louder as his unspoken thoughts hung in the air.

Rose picked up her phone and found the pictures she had taken in Nigel's room. "Please don't ask me how I got these, but I think they might help."

The DCI flicked through the images. "I'll get prints made. Rose, you can't keep doing this. You obviously broke into the man's hotel suite for God's sake."

Rose raised her eyebrows. "But they're helpful. Right?"

The DCI didn't answer and clicked on the photograph of the box of coins, unwilling to admit that they might help. Nigel was a collector, the symposium was about coins and medals. Nigel would have brought coins with him to show or sell, but there had been too many hordes of valuable coins turned up recently. He pressed on the phone to enlarge the image of the box. "Well, I'll be …" he said as he made sense of the marks in the wood on the top of the box.

"Rose, the box, when you first saw it, what did you think you were going to find inside it?"

"I don't know. Why?"

"These marks, they're not very clear on the image." He handed her back the phone.

Rose squinted, screwing up her good eye, "I didn't notice them, I was in a hurry, what do you think they are?"

"Look."

Rose peered closely at the enlarged image, she could clearly see what was carved into the top of the box. *Blut und Ehre. JWB.*

"JWB, wait, those initials were on one of the drawings we found at Terpsichore. *Blud und Ehre*, Blood and Honour, was a Nazi slogan. Do you think Callum is involved with the Neo-Nazi protests? That the coins were stolen or connected to the ones we heard those men talking about at the cottage?"

The DCI held up his hand. "I don't know Rose, but this stays here, between you and me, understand?"

Rose leaned forward. "So, I was a little bit useful then, on my visit to Chester?"

"Icarus ... I warned you Rose."

Rose smiled. "Yep, Detective Chief Inspector, you surely did."

Rose made her way back into the centre of Edinburgh, the tourist shops would still be open. She wanted to see if she could identify the shop that sold the pack of cards that the Queen of Diamonds was from. She knew finding whoever had bought it was like searching for a needle in a haystack. She had planned to go to an AA meeting but her meeting with the DCI had raised more questions. Why did Nigel have a box with those initials and that horrible saying on it? Rose went into the tourist shops at Waverley Station. But none of the packs they sold matched the back of the one she had received.

The manager at the last shop Rose visited picked up a catalogue they ordered cards from. There were hundreds of different styles, but he pointed to a set that matched the back of the card Rose showed him. We do normally carry them, but we're out of stock.

"Do you know if that was recent, or when the last pack might have been sold?"

The manager scrolled through a spreadsheet on the computer. "The last pack was sold yesterday, looks like a cash transaction."

"Is there any way you would know who bought them, or the time?"

"We have a camera, but look, you're not police and well ... Why is it important?"

Rose thought for a moment, she hoped her story was plausible. "A card from a pack like this was shoved under my door, I'm just trying to find out if I have a stalker or something, the police can't do anything unless I have more information."

He hesitated, "That sucks, my girlfriend had a stalker once, it really creeped her out. OK let me take a look later, it's not very likely that I'll be able to spot them though, the shop can get pretty busy, and it's mostly focused on the door area."

"Thanks. Here's my number, you can text me if you do find anything. Appreciate it."

"No bother, I'll take a look later, once we're closed."

Rose left the shop and made her way up The Scotsman Steps up to North Bridge and The Scotsman Hotel. She knew the police would have searched his room, but there was a chance that the book was still there, maybe the letter was too. The reception area was busy, and she needed a valid key card to take her upstairs to the guest rooms. She waited by the lifts. As a young couple heading upstairs for what looked like a night of drunken passion passed her, the woman dropped her key card. Rose snatched it up and followed them to the lift.

"Which floor?" asked Rose as the couple staggered through the doors.

"Oh thank you, four please." The woman giggled, burying her head into the man's shoulder "I'm a wee bit ..."

Rose laughed and nodded. "You're having a great evening."

As the lift closed Rose looked at the key card, she had read somewhere that any key card could get you into a room of a hotel due to a flaw in the system. She just hoped it would work. There was no sign of police presence on the fifth floor and the door to the room Chris had used was closed. It wasn't where he was killed so the room was not taped off as a crime scene. Rose tried the key card, no luck. Clearly no flaw with this system. She was about to give up when she noticed a very slim gap between the door and the frame. Rose pushed the card through, jiggled it, and heard the lock shoot back. She looked back over her shoulder, no one was there, and the lift had long closed, she quickly slipped into the room.

The room had been made up, but all of Chris's personal belongings were still there. The Dante book was on the bedside table. Rose picked it up and put it in her bag. She looked through the pockets of the jackets hanging in the wardrobe. The cloak and bag he used for the show were not there and Rose knew he would have been wearing the cloak. There was nothing in any of his pockets and she was about to leave when she heard someone outside the door. The sound of a key card being inserted. Rose froze, there was nowhere to hide and no escape, how on earth was she going to explain why she was there?

Chapter Nine

DCI Chatterton had just said goodbye to Rose when Donna phoned. "OK, I can meet you there in half an hour. Thanks Donna."

The DCI looked over his notes about the boy Trixie had found on the steps. What was this all about? His earlier conversation with Donna had mended fences and he was glad to be able to share the load with someone who had known him earlier in his life - before his wife had left and he had become sour. Donna told him her boss was open to sharing information, given there was now a DNA connection to the remains of the young woman found at Terpsichore and one of the murder victims in Edinburgh.

"What else do you know about what might have happened to your girl, and who she was?" asked the DCI. They had met at the lab and then driven out to Portobello. The cafe was quiet and private enough to have a conversation.

"She was reported missing by her mother at least three years ago. They're not sure what happened to her yet, and honestly if it hadn't been for the screening being done at the same lab, I doubt we'd be this far. It made more sense to use the specialist bone testing facilities in Edinburgh than shipping them to London. It was the lab who spotted the connection. We wouldn't have picked it up, well not this quickly anyway. It was fast for a tox report, I mean usually it takes at least four weeks, but this came back in a couple of days because of your guy and what they were processing.

"So, Devon and this girl are brother and sister?"

"Looks like it."

"In which case, maybe Rose was onto something. Our latest victim was on the scene when Devon's body was found. He called for help, or rather he told the girl, Rose's assistant, to call. Rose started seeing him after that, then she found a piece of paper in his hotel room with the name of the cottage written on it. Terpsichore. She also said she saw a letter addressed to Devon in Canada, but she didn't know what the letter said. We found nothing like that when we searched the room. Rose thought he had to be involved somehow."

Donna swiped her hand across the table, "What is it about her? Have you asked yourself why she was really at the cottage, then in Chester? Now you say she was having an affair with your last victim. Her assistant 'found' the first victim? I'd say she should be on your suspect list, I'm certainly adding her to ours."

The DCI shook his head. "Rose isn't involved criminally, Donna, but she has been behaving stupidly, poking into police business. It's not the first time."

"What do you mean?"

"Rose helped solve a big case in Edinburgh, nearly getting herself killed in the process."

"And you're soft on her."

"As if. Behave Donna. Rose is at least a quarter of a century younger than this old dog."

"Has there been anyone since ..." Donna paused. When the DCI's wife left, he had all but fallen apart. She knew what that was like, and she had wanted to repay him for helping her through suspension and demotion. The DCI's career trajectory went seriously off course, after he started drinking. They had stayed in touch after her transfer, but then came his big crash, the botched investigation when a child died, and he'd refused her help. He was definitely not the man she had first met. He was gentler, a good listener, but perhaps he was too soft, lost his touch for seeing people for what they really were.

The DCI let Donna's question fall without answering, as he sipped his coffee, staring out towards the open seascape. There had been women he liked. But after what happened in Northampton, the demotion and then the transfer North he had chosen singleness. Was it because they had both experienced a life changing fall that he cared so much about what happened to Rose, he wondered?

He looked back at Donna. She still had the same dark hair, cut into a bob, that she'd had when they first worked together. There were flecks of silver now, but not many and it didn't look as though she dyed it. But that was all there was of the old Donna, despite her criticism of Rose, whatever had driven her when she was younger had gone, she no longer looked like she would trample over everyone to get where she wanted to go. The drive that had proven to be both attractive and fatal for her professionally and personally. "You?" he asked. "You didn't marry?"

"Almost, three times in fact," she grinned. "I'm a collector of proposals, but I can't seem to get myself to the altar."

"Anyone I know?"

"No one from when we worked together, I thought, well, it seems silly now and I get it. You were raw, bruised from your wife leaving like that."

"And you were out of my league." The DCI said, looking directly into her eyes. "Still are."

Donna smiled and reached her hand across the table. "Perhaps it was the other way round, I have never worked with anyone quite like you since."

DCI Chatteron leaned in, responding to her hand and placing hers between both of his. He had just summoned up the courage to say something he had wanted to say some years before, when her phone rang.

"DI Gibbs," she answered curtly.

The DCI watched her nodding as she spoke, scribbling in the book she pulled out of her bag. "OK, I'll be right there." She put the phone down. "You're never going to believe this."

"Tell me."

"They've traced where those coins they found were from."

"I don't understand why, whoever burned down the cottage, left something so valuable behind?

"Me neither. They were well hidden though. Alongside the body, under a concrete patio. I suppose we do have your Rose to thank for that, if she hadn't told us what she had overheard about remains, it's unlikely we would have dug it up. Are you coming?"

The DCI nodded and followed her out of the cafe. His curiosity was piqued but he also realised he was disappointed that the evening had ended so abruptly and not in the direction that it had seemed to be going before the phone call. Had he been mistaken about the messages he thought she had been giving him? It was already seven pm. Given the day, the sunset from where they had been eating would be spectacular too. Pity, he thought, as he weaved his way through the traffic towards the motorway.

Chapter Ten

Rose ducked into the bathroom as she heard the suite door open. She was shaking, remembering a different time when she had been trapped in a room from which there had seemingly been no escape. Except she had. "Breathe Rose," she told herself, clutching the book she had lifted from the bedside table to her chest.

"You go through the wardrobe, I'll do the drawers." Came a man's voice.

"Do you really want to take all his belongings, I mean, what's the point?" Rose immediately recognised Sam's voice.

"We're not taking anything apart from that book. I don't know when he took it, but ..." Rose could hear drawers and cupboards being opened and slammed shut. She was crouched down inside the bathtub, behind the floor length shower curtain. The door to the bathroom opened. She gulped in air, holding herself as still and silently as she could.

"If it's not here, maybe he gave it to that girl after all. If the police got hold of it ... It doesn't matter, they won't realise."

"What are you talking about?"

"Oh for god's sake Sam, stay with it. Anyway, it looks like we're done. It's not here. The police can do whatever they do to dead people's stuff. I don't want any of it. Damn waste of a trip this has been. I need to get back to New York as soon as possible, but we should split up, you'll have to deal with that other business on your own."

"What do you mean?"

"Who do you think I mean?"

Rose shivered at the tone of his voice.

"But what about the funeral, won't it look strange if you're not there? Our other plans?"

"As of now there are no other plans, Sam. Keep your stupid mouth shut. That girl recognising your face has caused enough trouble."

Rose heard the door close after them. Her head was spinning. What was he planning to organise from New York? He had called her 'that girl' twice. Did that mean he didn't know who she really was? Rose waited a few minutes just in case they returned, her upper legs were throbbing from the squat, a reminder about the state of her body and lack of exercise. Rose stretched herself upwards and stepped back through the double shower curtain. She opened the book and flipped through the pages. Where was that letter? She knew it was no use but in that moment she wished Chris had told her the truth. What was it that he had had to do that had got him killed? She checked her watch, it was already past seven, Rose took the lift down to reception and slipped behind one of the palms when she saw Sam and Nigel at the reception desk, talking to one of the staff. It was too noisy to hear what they were saying. She recognised the black case Nigel was gripping, from the hotel room in Chester, she saw the two Louis Vuitton cases, sitting on a trolley behind where Sam was standing. Had they been planning to stay here? Rose checked her phone for flights to New York. What she had heard was hardly going to bring DCI Chatterton rushing over, she needed to know more.

"Sam, Nigel, hello," Rose said, stepping out of her hiding place into the main foyer.

"Libby, what are you doing here?" Sam looked surprised to see her.

"Oh, just passing through, can I buy you both a drink in the Bistro Bar?"

"That would be lovely. We're just trying to find a hotel for tonight, our plans have changed Libby, because of ..." She stopped speaking and looked at Nigel. "We're heading out to the airport tomorrow."

"Oh, really, where are you going?" Rose asked, hoping her face conveyed surprise.

"Home, business." Nigel snapped. "Sorry Libby, another time. Let's go Sam."

"Sorry, honestly Libby, aren't men grouchy?" Her laugh reminded Rose of all the times she had tried to cover up for her ex. Troy when he had been rude and put her down in front of other people. Trying to fake togetherness when all she had felt was pain.

"What time is your flight? If it's tomorrow, surely you have time for a bite to eat, it's such a lovely evening." Rose knew she was pushing things, but she wanted to keep them in her sights, let DCI Chatterton know what she had just overheard.

"Thanks for the invitation, *Libby*, but it's really not a good time."

Rose knew from the way he had emphasised her name and his facial expressions that he knew who she really was. Had Chris told him?

"Look, can we just talk somewhere else Nigel, you clearly know I knew your brother."

"You knew Chris, Libby?" Rose saw Nigel pull on Sam's arm, to shut her up.

"Do you have something that belongs to Chris, Libby, or should I call you Rose?"

Rose, startled by the open accusation, hesitated. "Errr, no ..."

"Let's talk, Rose. Come to our hotel at 9pm. We're staying at The Sheraton. I've got calls to make."

"I don't think I'll do that Nigel."

"Will someone tell me what's going on?" said Sam.

"Fine. Goodbye then Rose. Sam, come on." Nigel grabbed Sam's arm roughly and waved to the porter standing by. "We need a taxi. Bring these bags."

Rose watched the porter trundle after them with the suitcases and then turned to the receptionist. "I was a friend of one of your guests, Mr Foley. Can you tell me what's happening to his belongings? Have the police finished with his room?" The girl shrugged and beckoned to her colleague, whispering.

They both stared at Rose, but it was the second girl who spoke. "The manager is the one to ask, but she's busy right now, a wedding party. If you leave your name. His brother has just left, we both saw you speaking to him." The girl indicated her colleague who Rose had first spoken to.

"It's OK, I'll call the police, ask them myself."

DCI Chatterton didn't pick up. Rose left him a message, asking him to meet her as soon as possible.

By the time he returned her call she was already waiting in the reception area of The Sheraton. He arrived shortly afterwards and listened intently as she filled him in on what she had overheard. Damn her interfering and interrupting his evening he thought unreasonably as he listened.

"Rose, you dragged me here to tell me that you broke into a dead man's room while his brother was in there legitimately, with my permission, looking for something that belonged to a member of his family. An item which you took."

"I had to. It was a spur of the moment response. Look, when I went to Chester, I wasn't expecting to see the woman who modelled for Callum Blackwater with Nigel Foley, and Nigel was pretty annoyed when I asked him if Sam had been Callum Blackwater's model. Now he is going back to New York, and she is supposed to take care of someone. I don't know how, or who, but it was the way he said it, it honestly made my blood run cold. How did you identify Chris Foley so quickly by the way, if his brother was in Chester?"

"We already knew who he was."

"How, was he a suspect?"

The DCI rolled his eyes. “Stop. Rose. This book, why did you take it, or think it was important?”

“I don’t know. I thought maybe Chris had put the letter back inside it.”

DCI Chatteron sat on one of the couches and opened the book. After flicking through the pages, he closed his eyes and gave out a huge sigh.

“Do you have any idea what it’s about?” Rose asked quietly, sitting opposite him.

“Rose, I have no idea and I have no reason to go and ask Nigel Foley and his girlfriend about their plans, other than to return this book you stole.”

“Please don’t do that. Nigel invited me to talk to him and what about that letter? I could go up, see what I can find out?”

“No Rose. That might put you in harm's way and as much as you are annoying the heck out of me right now, I don’t want …”

“So, you do think there is something. And if he goes to New York, you will lose an opportunity to ask him about … well I am not sure what, but he knows something important.”

“Exactly Rose. We don’t know, you don’t know, and as I have said, time after time, procedure is essential. You running about breaking into hotel suites and pretending to be someone else, isn’t procedure. What you’ve been up to is illegal. The only person I could arrest right now is you! Surely you realise that.”

Rose put her finger to her mouth and ducked down as Nigel Foley came out of the lift with a Louis Vuitton suitcase and the black business case. The DCI turned round and motioned to Rose to stay where she was. He stood up, facing Nigel Foley with his back to Rose. Nigel did not notice either of them, he was clearly intent on catching the eye of the doorman. The doorman offered to help with the larger case, but Nigel shook his head and strode out to the waiting taxi.

"What are you going to do?" hissed Rose, still crouching by the sofa.

"I'm probably going to regret this, but I am going to find out where he's heading."

Rose stood up and watched the inspector stride after Nigel, who was already in the back of a taxi.

Rose went over to the reception desk, "Sorry, I left my bag in my room, locked myself out. Mrs Foley."

"Yes, Madam, which room number?"

"Sorry," Rose pulled out her phone and then started speaking in a loud voice. "Oh darling, reception won't give me the room key, I'm locked out, can you speak to them please." Rose handed her phone over to the reception clerk, hoping Rob would play along. He did. Seconds later the clerk handed her a freshly activated key in a wallet with the room number.

"Sorry madam, I wasn't trying to be ..."

"Oh, no, I'm sure. Thank you so much," said Rose, interrupting the apology and smiling generously.

Rose tapped on the door of the suite.

"Who is it?"

"It's Libby, Rose, I changed my mind about coming to talk to Nigel."

Sam opened the door. She was dressed in expensive casual active wear and holding a large glass of wine."

"Nigel's popped out. He shouldn't be long. Come in."

Rose smiled at how easily the lie tripped off her tongue. It was an enviable skill, albeit, in her case Rose thought, possibly a dangerous one.

"Wine?" Sam gestured with her glass.

"I don't thank you, but tea, or coffee would be great. Silly question, given everything that's just happened, especially Nigel's brother being murdered, but how are you feeling?" asked Rose as they settled into the armchairs facing each other.

"Numb," said Sam.

"Why did you lie to me about who you were in Chester Rose?"

So, this was the game she was planning to play, thought Rose as she considered her answer.

"I felt a bit bad about spying on Chris. I wanted to find out more about him, meeting his brother, well it was pretty dumb of me wasn't it."

"You created quite a row between us, when you told him you knew I had modelled for Callum. Nigel doesn't like the association. Not good for his investors."

Rose had to hand it to Sam, she was cool as a cucumber.

"So where is Nigel?"

"Oh, he forgot he had to sign some papers. He won't be long. I already told you."

"No problem. Do you know why he wanted to talk to me? Was it about Callum?"

Sam tipped the glass back, hiding her face momentarily. "Callum, Callum Blackwater? I doubt it. I don't know, he didn't tell me."

"Well, as Nigel's not here, what was Callum like? According to the news he's missing.

Sam shrugged. "Callum is a Jekyll and Hyde. One minute he is charming, happy go lucky, the next he can be a right pig to be honest. As for what's happened to him, I don't know, and I don't care. I never want to see him again. He's a thief and a fraudster."

"What do you mean?"

"He was a con man. Sold paintings and then pretended they were by someone else, I thought you would have picked that up from the news."

"Yeah, I did, but it sounded like there was more to it than that. Wasn't there also a model who disappeared?"

"How do you know about her?"

"Umm, it was on the news.

"I doubt if Callum had anything to do with that or killed her, if that's what you mean. Callum was a coward. Unless it was an accident. He would definitely cover up an accident, but not by himself. Someone else would have to have helped."

"You said Callum *was* ..."

"Yeah, because I haven't seen him since I left the job. I didn't mean he wasn't still around." Sam's face flushed when she spoke.

So, that lie was not so easy, Rose observed. Did that mean Callum was dead? She checked her watch. It was already close to midnight, and she was shattered, but she didn't want to leave, risking Sam taking off before she had worked out what Sam's plans were. Sam had no idea that Rose knew she and Nigel planned to travel separately. Rose pinged Trixie a text.

Sorry to ask, but can you come early and make a start on morning baking? Batters are done. I'll be there as soon as I can.

A questioning emoji appeared almost instantly and then an OK.

Thanks Trixie. Promise I'll make it up to you.

Yes Rose, you will. Night.

Rose smiled at the gif that followed. A couple of mice laying on a large bed on a patchwork quilt. Their tails were curled together in the shape of a heart.

"Good for you Trixie," Rose murmured.

"Trixie?" asked Sam. "Cute name."

"Yes, without her help these last few days, I think my business would have sunk."

"What do you do Rose, as you're not really a journalist."

"I run a shop, we sell muffins, treats, baked goods, it's how I met Chris."

"Really?"

"Yes, really."

Sam smiled. "I thought you met him because she was the one who found Devon."

"You know about that?

"Well yes, not until earlier though. Nigel told me. It seems you and your little Trixie thought Chris had murdered him."

"No, that's not quite right."

The two women sat in silence. Sam fiddling with her jewellery looked uncomfortable. Rose decided to risk opening up a conversation.

"Sam, what's going on? Is Nigel making you do things that you don't want to do? I know what that's like."

"Why would you think that about Nigel? I'm fine, I can do what I want when I want."

"Sorry, it's just that I know you were in Berwick upon Tweed."

"So?"

"It's where Callum has a cottage. It burned down, there was a woman buried there."

"I don't know anything about that. I went to Berwick to buy coins for Nigel."

"Why there though?"

"The dealer lives there. It's nothing more sinister than a coincidence. Honestly Rose, stop behaving like you're in some sort of mystery production, playing Miss Marple."

"I'm sorry, that's not what I'm doing. But, well, can I be honest Sam? I really liked Chris, perhaps we could talk about him. How well did you know him?"

Sam smiled, "Sure, perhaps there are things it would be good to talk to someone about. How about I make us both a tea, there's some herbal, or hot chocolate. I find it helps me relax."

"Thanks. It would be good to talk to you, until Nigel gets back, it's late, he's been gone for quite a while. I'll just let my friend know that I'll be back late." Rose pulled out her phone and sent a text to the DCI.

I'm with Sam.

Chapter Eleven

Rose groaned at the sound of knocking on the door of the suite. The room was pitch black and her head was thumping, when had she fallen asleep and where was Sam? Whoever was knocking was getting louder, more impatient. Rose stumbled over to the door and flicked on the light. It was the DCI.

"You look rough Rose, not a good night?" The DCI snipped as Rose unlocked the door and let him in.

"What time is it?"

"Almost six, what were you thinking?"

"That I was helping. Are you alright? You look pretty rough too."

He sighed. "It's this case, it's a mess, too many loose ends, victims that don't fit with each other and I'm also a bit short on sleep."

"I'll make some coffee. What happened to Nigel? Are you planning to talk to Sam?"

"Yes, and thanks, coffee would be great. I thought about sending a uniform, but I decided it would be better if I came - once I realised you were still here. Do you mind telling her I'm here? My knocking seems not to have disturbed her?"

"Of course." Rose started the coffee maker and crossed the room to the bedroom. She tapped gently, then louder, but there was no reply. "Sam" she called out, before she opened the door. "Inspector!"

The DCI strode across the room towards Rose, she had thrown the door wide open, there was no one there. The Louis Vuitton case and her handbag had gone.

"How could you just let her leave without telling me?"

"I ... I didn't, the last I saw of her was sitting opposite me, she was pretending to wait up with me for NIgel. I didn't hear her leave, except ..." Rose looked at the cup on the coffee table in front of the sofa. "She must have put something in the herbal tea."

"I'll make a call. She's probably getting on a later flight to New York, she didn't fly out with Nigel. His plane left at 6am. I'm going to need you to come to the station and make a statement about what she told you. Rose, are you playing me? Did you really not know she was gone?"

"Honestly, I didn't and I would have at least warned you. Do you want to take the cup, examine the dregs?"

The DCI nodded and waved his hand in the air as he phoned the front desk. "This suite must be locked until further notice. Please ask the manager to see that nothing is disturbed. I'll need checkout information, credit cards etc."

"What are you looking for?"

"I have no idea. What exactly was Sam doing when you arrived?"

"She was relaxing, drinking wine. It didn't look like she was getting ready to go anywhere."

"OK, well, as Nigel is on his way to New York, I'm going to assume she's on her way there as well."

"What about the ferry tickets and the booking from Amsterdam? I sent you photos."

"Good point. Let's go to the station, I can get things moving easier from there."

Rose sent Trixie and Rob a text.

Sorry, I'm going to have to go to the station with DCI Chatterton and give another statement. I'll fill you in asap. Can you both manage?

Trixie sent a text back straight away.

You need to buy ingredients. Everything's ok today but then we're out. What about the stall? I can't do both.

Rose sighed. She could feel the frustration in Trixie's subtext.

Sorry, I'm on it. I'll be there as soon as I can. I promise.

"How long do you think we'll be doing my statement I mean? My business is falling apart."

The DCI looked up from the desk. "Well Rose, if you hadn't interfered, you wouldn't have that problem."

Rose wanted to fight back, but she could see from his face that the DCI was unlikely to see anything from her point of view this morning. She took a breath and with her fists clenched mumbled, "I'm sorry."

By the time Rose arrived at Muffins on Morrison the shop was mobbed. Rob was behind the counter and Trixie was doing her best to keep on top of baking and making sure they had things to sell.

"Rose, we cannae dae this without more help. It's nae working." Trixie wiped her hand across her forehead as she spoke. "And nae more *Ah'm sorry*. Fix it Rose."

Rose bit her lip, she was feeling rubbish and she knew Trixie was right. She had created the problem. She wanted to find out what had happened to Chris, and she couldn't let it go. But she would need to do things differently if her business was going to survive.

"Okay Trixie. Take a break, I'll take over baking from here, then I'll do the shopping. You are right, we're going to need to hire some help."

Trixie opened her mouth to say something, banter back, but changed her mind as she recognised the familiar look of determination cross Rose's face.

"Rose ah dinnae ... Ah'm worried aboot ye?"

Rose held up her hand. "It's ok, I'm ok. If I hadn't become involved with Chris, I could probably just take a step back. But I can't do that. I feel responsible. I feel I've got to put right what I messed up."

Trixie knew there was no point trying to rationalise with Rose. It was obvious that she couldn't possibly have known the mind of an as yet unknown murderer. Her job now was to make sure Muffins on Morrison survived.

"Ah'll run a Facebook post for help with the stall. Ah can manage tae run the shop, with Rob's help. If we get someone good tae dae the stall. It should pay for itself. Och, sorry Rose. Ah thought it would be good for business, nae a burden."

"The stall was a good idea, Trixie, still is. We are in good shape. Don't worry about it, you've done well. Just please try to understand that I have to do this."

"Och, ah'll nae be mithering on. Just take care. I wish ah had run away when ah saw that boy on The Steps."

"I will take care and you didn't run away because it wasn't the right thing to do. But it's because of how you reacted afterwards and what happened last time that I don't want to involve you again. Now, let me get these muffins in the oven or we'll have nothing to sell."

It was after 6pm by the time Rose returned from the cash and carry. She was deep in thought when she heard someone knocking on the door at the front of the shop. It was a man in his early thirties. He was disheveled as if he had been sleeping rough.

"Sorry, we're closed." Rose mouthed through the glass and pointed at the sign.

He bent down and called out through the letterbox. "Rose please, it's Callum Blackwater."

"Callum?"

He was standing again, nodding as she spoke his name.

Rose paused. After falling for Sam's trick last night how could she be sure she wasn't being fooled again.

Cautiously she unlocked the door. "Why are you here?

"Sam said that I could trust you. That you wanted to help, to find out what had happened to Devon, Chris and the others."

"I did. I do. But after last night Sam is the last person I'm about to trust."

"Look, you've got it all wrong. Sam and I. Please can I come in and explain?"

Rose paused, holding onto the door.

"Rose, I know this seems crazy, but I can tell you things, things that will help."

Rose's dander was up. "I'll listen to what you have to say, but I'm leaving the door unlocked and I'll not hesitate to call the police."

"OK, fair enough. But please don't tell the police until I've told you what I know. Then you can do what you like with the information."

Rose let him through the door and indicated to the table by the window. Rose justified the risk she was taking letting Callum into the shop. If Callum had information that could direct them to finding who killed Chris and the others, she would listen and then call the DCI. She regretted the tension that was festering between her and the DCI. He had taken a lot of convincing that Rose hadn't had anything to do with Sam leaving. But it was the DI from England who had really stirred things up.

Donna had tried to disguise her snippy comments as professional observations, but Rose saw through them and something else, Donna had her sights set on the DCI, did he know? Perhaps sexual frustration was what was making him grumpy these days? There were probably rules about investigations and bedrooms despite what happened on TV dramas.

"OK Callum, tell me why you are really here? And just so you know I'm really tired of all the BS and lies, so whatever you have to say it had better be the truth."

"I get it. Sam and I stayed in contact, Nigel didn't know. We met in Berwick, then she told me to hide somewhere in Edinburgh and wait. I've been sleeping rough in Queensferry until she called me earlier yesterday evening and told me to meet her. She was going to help me get away, we were going to fly out together, but then you turned up at her hotel, which put paid to that plan."

Rose frowned, that didn't tally with what Sam had said last night or what she had overheard Nigel say to Sam at The Scotsman. But she decided to let Callum spin his side of the story before she challenged it.

"Where were you planning to go?"

"We hadn't got that far, the first flight to anywhere and take it from there."

"Not much of a plan, but tell me your version of the story, Callum. Start at the beginning and don't leave anything out."

Callum pulled out a playing card from his pocket. "It all started with meeting him," he said as he turned over the top card. Rose squinted and examined the card more closely.

"The Joker," she said as she recognised the harlequin image. It was Oliver Moorcroft, Callum's angel investor.

"Yes, he really is, in more ways than one."

Chapter Twelve

"I'll make us both tea," said Rose, playing for time. She sent a text to Rob.

If I don't text you by 10pm please call the DCI. I'm at the shop.

"Thanks. And, sorry but do you have anything to eat?"

Rose made tea and brought over a plate of leftovers. Callum dove into the plate, clearly ravenous.

"So you've been sleeping rough? You look ..."

Callum interrupted her. "Yes, it's been almost a week. Look, what I'm about to tell you, doesn't reflect well on me and if I could turn back time I would."

"When did you go to Berwick?"?"

"The day I spoke to you on the phone. Oliver had told me to go to Terpsichore after things had hit the press about him until everything quietened down. When you called and sent me that picture from the prototype playing card I'd made, I called Oliver. He told me to lose my phone. By the time I got to Terpsichore, it was almost dawn. I saw someone was watching the place, so I left. Then I contacted Sam, she came to meet me at a hotel in Berwick."

"Why did you contact Sam? Sam said that she went to Berwick to get coins for Nigel."

"Yes, that was true, she did. Everything is probably going to make more sense if I go back to the end of my second year at Bath, before I met him," he pointed to the card.

Rose nodded. "Alright Callum, I'm listening."

"I was twenty-eight when I went to Bath, older than the rest of the students. It was thanks to my grandmother passing and the tiny inheritance that I was finally able to do what I'd dreamed of. She had offered to support me through art school years before, but I couldn't take her money, not while she was alive, it would have been too much pressure if I had failed. I became a landscaper, convinced her that it was my art. Breathing life into gardens and creating new wild spaces. She loved what I did with the cottage garden, it was the last thing she saw before she died.

It was the last day of my second year there, well after midnight. I wanted to see the end of year art exhibition one final time, before it opened. I often went to the studio at night to paint, so I knew my way into the locked building. I found the kaleidoscope of colour and wild shapes that filled my brain flowed more easily onto the canvas and papers after dark. I liked moulding the textures together until they fused, overlapping inks and oil paint under the glass atrium using the light of the moon or stars and sometimes lighted candles. Well, when the exhibition opened, I saw that all my paintings had already been marked sold. But, there had been no red dots on them the night before. I had no idea who Oliver Moorcroft was or that he had bought all of the paintings, until he invited me to meet him in London.

"We went for lunch at the Chelsea Arts Club. I could tell from the reception they gave him that he was pretty revered. He told me that he had buyers who would pay a lot of money for my work. I can still hear his words. *... and if you'll allow me to influence you a little, you will become very famous."* Callum mimicked the American accent. Then he handed me a sketchbook and asked if I was aware of the artist.

"The book was filled with rough sketches all signed by JWB. I knew immediately how rare and valuable it was. I asked him where he had got it and he said he was a collector who collected things."

Rose held up her hand to stop him. "So, you made copies from the book?"

"I didn't. He did and sent them to me. I don't know where they are now. Why?"

Rose pulled out her phone. "I saw them at Terpsichore." She showed Callum the pictures, "Are they the same ones?"

"Yes, yes they are. I don't know why they were there. I had them in London."

"Like you thought you had the set of playing cards?

"Yes, right," Callum frowned.

"Who is, or was JWB?"

"JWB was an artist from the late 1920's and early 1930''s. Actually, I knew about him from my grandmother, she worked as an undercover operative during the war.

JWB lived in Berlin. In the mid-thirties he became a very influential vocal supporter of Hitler. His later art that the Allies destroyed represented Hitler's visions of an Aryan society. His earlier art, like these images, were different, you can see they are very bold, almost shockingly daring. They focus on women as powerful and strong. By the end of the war JWB was wanted on serious charges for war crimes by the Allies. He killed himself when the war ended. I couldn't believe I was holding a whole book of his early sketches. The drawings were ideas and concepts that he had never painted and, despite knowing his later political beliefs, I liked them. Oliver told me that my work reminded him of JWB, and what he might have gone on to do, if he hadn't stopped painting. He then said that if I agreed to use the sketches and paint them, they could one day be worth even more than the book itself.

"I told him I didn't copy other artists. That what I paint is from within me and that I didn't support or believe in JWB's brand of so-called philosophy once he became a Nazi. But Oliver still managed to hook me. Reverse psychology I suppose.

"He told me he wished me luck with my career. That life can be expensive and difficult for a starving artist having to search for commissions. And he already had buyers lined up, I could create the paintings as JWB and still exhibit my own art. He told me he had even resold my paintings he had bought from the art exhibition to a collector. I knew what my Gran had left me wasn't going to take me far and he was right, getting anywhere as an unknown artist is pretty hard."

"I have no idea how Oliver came across my work before the exhibition, or when he detected my desperation. I guess everyone has a price, even artists.

"Only five of JWB's early original paintings exist, in two private collections, but they are never offered for exhibition. The British and Americans destroyed everything that JWB didn't burn. There is also a well-documented letter requesting JWB to paint Wallace Simpson. But JWB refused the commission, saying even though she was beautiful, she wasn't what he looked for in a model. He had always used the same model. When I asked Oliver how he would explain the new paintings, he told me not to worry. They would all be going to private collectors. The work wouldn't be seen publicly. I only learned later, the real scam was nothing to do with paintings.

"The more Oliver spoke about the possibilities, the more intoxicated I became. If I put up any arguments, he always had an answer, the lies came easily, and he spun me well. Then, when he could see I was his, Oliver pulled out papers for me to sign along with a cheque for £75,000. The advance took my breath away and without considering the legal implications or even consulting a lawyer I didn't hesitate. I grabbed his Montblanc pen and signed. Isn't that mad? He had known, even before I sat down, that I would sign.

"A few days later, after the cheque was cashed, Oliver called me. He had a request. I was to play a practical joke on another student at Bath. He told me the boy had broken his niece's heart and the prank was a harmless pay back. He also told me that, if I did this, his niece would agree to model for the paintings. He showed me her photograph. She was perfect. Beautiful.

"When I told him, I was worried about the prank, that it didn't seem harmless, he sent someone to talk to me. I soon realised I had no choice but to do Oliver's bidding. This isn't an excuse, but I entered a kind of myopia, I agreed to whatever Oliver asked me to do. Then I started drinking to blot out my conscience and escape reality with other drugs. It was a lethal concoction. And later, I found out the lethal dose was not mine. It was the young student who had agreed to help model for the practical joke, and I did nothing about it." Callum paused his story. Hung his head "I told you this story reflected badly on me."

"You're telling the wrong person if you're looking for sympathy," Rose's reply was cold, she was finding it hard to listen to Callum.

He nodded. "I get it. Well, after I photographed her, I never saw her again, no one did. Her mother caused quite a stink because she thought no one cared, and in a way no one seemed to. It was during an argument, when I tried to refuse another of his so-called jokes that Oliver told me the girl was dead and she was buried at Terpsichore."

Rose gasped and put her hand to her mouth. "What was the argument about, why did he tell you about the girl then?"

"His niece had modelled for another painting. Not one of the one's for Oliver. I sold it, without Oliver being involved. The buyer made prints and used them for some invitations and the image had gone quite public. Oliver and his niece were furious. I told him I wanted to leave. Free myself from a form of paid enslavement. When he told me about the girl I knew I had no escape route left. The next day Oliver arrived at the studio with Sam and told me she would take his niece's place as the model. She had the same fine bone structure, and her figure was similar. Full busted with slim hips and long legs. She was a perfect replacement, but he warned me against using her to model for anything else.

"So, Oliver knew Sam, before she knew Nigel?"

"Yes. I think she met Nigel about a year later. Then, after Sam left things changed and Oliver dragged me further into his trap. I found out that the paintings were really just a cover for a black-market trade in valuable coins, precious stones and ancient medals. They were taped between the canvas and the frame. Only a professional collector or a framer would know what to look for. Oliver said there had been a problem with one of the shipments, it was held up at a border somewhere and he needed to streamline things. I couldn't refuse. I was in too deep, no one would believe I hadn't been part of the whole thing right from the start. And, of course, there was also the body of the girl at Terpsichore. Oliver always had the upper hand."

Callum paused.

Rose watched him carefully. His hands were trembling as he finished the mug of tea. How much of his story was credible, she wondered? He hadn't mentioned anything about the playing cards, except for showing her the Joker. Why would Oliver choose to have his face on that card?

"You look like you have questions about what I have told you so far."

"Yeah, yeah I do. Your version of events is quite different to what Sam told me."

"Yeah, she told me that she'd said I am a Jekyll and Hyde. It was supposed to ... I don't know, until ..."

"Until what?"

Callum bit his lips, "I wasn't supposed to say."

"Too late now, look I meant it when I said no more BS Callum. If you want my help and you really are a victim in all this, you have to be straight with me."

"Sam told Chris she had a call when she was in Chester. It was a man, demanding to know where I was. He scared the living daylights out of her, told her he would expose her as my model. Chris said he would help her. Sam said she didn't want to tell Nigel, because he didn't know we had kept in touch."

"Wait, why did Sam go to Chris? That doesn't make sense."

"I don't know, she said Chris had helped her in the past."

"And Sam said she had no idea who this man who called her was?"

"No. But it's the sort of thing Oliver does, knows things he shouldn't know. As if someone is feeding him information."

"Nigel?"

"I don't know. I was gutted when Sam told me she had met Nigel, that she was planning to stop modelling and live with him. I didn't see much of her after that, and I've never even met him."

"Where did she cross paths with Nigel? And why didn't Sam leaving you, bother Oliver?"

"I have no idea. Sam didn't know anything about what was going on, although she did overhear me row on the phone with Oliver once. I liked Sam, and by that time I had enough roughs and reference points to create any of the paintings. Pretty much any model could have stood in just for sizing and shadows by the time she left."

"Do you know why someone would have delivered a playing card to me, the Queen of Diamonds?"

Callum shook his head.

"Why did you create the prototype playing cards Callum?"

"It was Oliver's idea. It was a vanity project, he was the one who commissioned them. He was going to have a limited number of sets made up and give them as gifts to friends, but then he changed his mind. It must have been his niece who took the prototypes when she left. This mockup for the actual pack was all I had left, apart from the drawings, at least I hope none of the other drawings survived."

"Why?"

"Well after I created the prototypes and Oliver told me they were for him, he asked me to put symbols on the cards."

"What sort of symbols?"

"They were Nazi symbols."

Rose wrote down the words that she had seen on the box of coins. "Like this?"

"Yes, that was on the back of the cards."

Rose paused, then asked, "What's her name?"

"Who?"

"Oliver's niece, who you think took the prototypes."

"Lucia ..."

Rose frowned, something about the name struck a chord. "Where is Sam now?"

"She's heading to get on a ferry."

"Does Nigel know where she is?"

"Yes. But obviously he doesn't know that I am meeting her, or that she's helping me. She said he needed her to sell some of his coins, she's meeting a buyer."

Rose thought about the conversation she had overheard at The Scotsman. It could make sense, but surely Nigel had used the word who, not what, that he wanted Sam to deal with?

"Sam could have told me all this last night. Instead, she put me to sleep for goodness sake."

"Yes. She's sorry about that and I am too, for lying earlier about the flights. Sam said you could be trusted to tell the police the truth. That you had influence somehow. Sam and me, we haven't done anything wrong."

"Apart from covering up a murder and assisting a smuggling operation. No, nothing wrong at all. It would be better if you told the police, surely. I can come with you There's a DCI - he pulled all the stops out for me once, so I could get justice. I was in prison for fraud, I hadn't done it. But it took time to prove I was innocent and DCI Chatterton helped clear up that record."

"I can't take that chance Rose, sorry."

"Which ferry are you both getting?"

Callum shook his head, “No, Rose, not until I know we are both safe, out of the country. If Oliver finds me, he will kill me, and probably Sam too, when he realises she’s helped me and I told her about the girl. Sam shouldn’t even go back to New York, now he’s there.”

“Callum, what about the fire at your cottage? Who did that?”

“I’m sure it was Oliver. Although I’m surprised about the coins. Oliver would never leave them behind without good reason. The game might be up for him publicly, but he’s like teflon, and I’m sure whatever sticks, it will be to someone else.”

“So why do you think he wants to kill you now, after all he’s in New York. He’s already set you up.”

“Yes, but I know too much. He will want to make sure I keep my mouth shut, I asked too many questions and in the end, I didn’t do what he told me. The last shipment that went belly up, it was worth over five million. There were three paintings on their way to Turks and Caicos via Santiago and the shipment was seized in Santiago. He might think I had something to do with the seizure.”

Rose pulled a notebook out of her back pocket and flipped it open to one of the maps she had drawn.

“What's that?”

“It’s a map of what’s been happening. It’s how I think. I create routes to make connections to things that don’t make sense or appear to be connected.”

“Impressive, where did you learn to do that?”

“RAF, before the sight gremlins got me.”

“What do you mean?”

"I'm totally blind in this eye, and the other one, well it's holding up, but the prognosis isn't great."

"I couldn't tell."

"No, well I've learned how to not stare like a cyclops when I'm listening. Look Callum, let's just go to the police. I know you think you are safer running, but I'm not sure that's really true and, Sam. Are you sure she really didn't know anything?"

"Yes, positive."

"It's quite the story. I am not sure anyone is going to believe me if I repeat what you've told me to be honest."

Rose looked at her map, "Despite everything you have said, however much I try there's no way I can connect Oliver to the murders. For one thing he couldn't have been in Edinburgh and New York at the same time."

"Well, he probably wouldn't get his hands dirty. I told you, he has people."

"Where is Lucia, his niece, do you know?"

"She was engaged to some academic, he was at Cambridge, I think. Last time I saw her was in a television commercial. She is beautiful but, in my opinion, she has the acting chops of a goat."

Callum checked the time. "I need to go. Rose, I promise you, I don't have anything to do with the murders. I've done a lot of things I am not proud of. But I hope telling you this will help to start to put that right."

His reasoning was illogical, but Rose understood why he thought what he did. She had been there herself. The DCI had been right, there were too many loose ends and victims. Was Callum really safer with Sam? Was Nigel somehow allied with Oliver through Sam?

"One more thing, at Terpsichore, in an out-building was there a freezer? It looked like something of that size had been moved."

"There wasn't a freezer. There was an old trunk though, it was huge, custom made by my grandfather."

"Why would Oliver move it from there, if he was trying to destroy everything at the cottage, frame you?"

"I don't know. I haven't opened it for years, it was full of old junk. I never bothered with it. But then one thing I did learn from Oliver, when I saw some of the things he asked me to hide, is that what looks like just junk can turn out to be very valuable."

"True, when was Oliver last there, that you know of?"

"The last time I know for sure he was there was just after I graduated. He threw me a party, Lucia was there too. How sick was that eh Rose. Throwing me a party where that poor girl was buried. But I think either he, or others who worked for him used Terpsichore. One time when I went up things had been moved around."

.oOo.

Rose sat staring out of the window after Callum left. It was almost 8.30pm and the sun was beginning her descent. There wouldn't be a spectacular sunset tonight she thought as she watched passers-by putting up umbrellas and donning plastic hats as they attempted to stay dry. The dreich evening reflected her own mood.

Rose's phone pinged. It was Rob.

Just saw the text. Damn it Rose what are you up to?

It's fine. Sorry. I'll explain tomorrow. Night and thanks for checking.

Despite her promise to Callum to wait until the next day, Rose knew she couldn't keep what she had learned from the DCI. There had already been too many secrets, and she wasn't about to contribute to the possibility of another death by keeping quiet.

Chapter Thirteen

"Well better late than never Rose. Thanks for calling and letting me know. You really have no idea where from and which ferry they are planning to take?" Despite the question Rose was relieved that the DCI had sounded genuine when he thanked her for the heads up about Callum and Sam's travel plans.

"My guess would be Newcastle, across to Holland. He wouldn't make it down to either Hull or Harwich for the night crossings, by the time he left here, but he may have been lying about taking a night crossing. And remember from the pictures I sent you, those tickets in Sam's bag, from before. She used the Harwich route then."

"You said Sam had a buyer for the coins?"

"According to Callum. He didn't say where in the world the buyer lives, but I looked at the profile of the dealer Sam said she met in Berwick. He also advertises a shop in Amsterdam and connections in Berlin and Zurich. And that got me thinking about the piece of furniture that was moved out of the outbuilding, at Terpsichore."

"What do you mean?"

"Well, remember I thought it could have been a freezer. Callum said it was probably a huge trunk that his grandfather had made, he thought it stored junk, but junk can also be treasure right? What if what was in there is getting shipped out to Oliver, somewhere in Europe, or even to New York?"

"Interesting thought. I'll talk to Donna. She'll have a busy morning ahead of her."

"Just don't tell her I mentioned about the trunk, or she'll come and have me arrested."

"Yes, Rose. You two do seem to have got off on the wrong foot."

"Whereas she appears to be quite taken with you DCI Chatterton." Rose knew she was taking a risk by teasing him so soon after their falling out.

"Rose, your imagination never fails to amaze," he chortled as he hung up.

Feeling guilty about the amount of work she had already piled onto Trixie recently, Rose started prepping the batters for the next day. She was looking through an old recipe book she had collected from a charity shop when she saw the inscription,' to my namesake Lucy with love from Auntie Lucia'. "Of course you idiot," she said aloud, "Lucia is the Latin spelling of Lucy."

Rose hurried to finish the prepping and get back to Corstorphine. As soon as she was inside the flat she fired up her laptop and started her research. According to Callum, Lucia, Oliver's niece, was an actor and model who had married an academic and moved to Cambridge. Lucy, the girl who was playing Alice, was also from Cambridge.

"Come on, come on," Rose muttered as the machine brought up a series of images. "Gotcha." she said as the picture of the same woman appeared across the multiple searches. Oliver's niece, Lucy, the actor cast as Alice and Lucia, wife of a history prof was one and the same. The similarity between her and Sam was remarkable. They could have been sisters, but Lucia had the edge. Rose hadn't seen her close up the day she had been taken away in an ambulance or before that, screaming for help, next to Josie, the Queen of Hearts, as she lay bleeding. Rose found coincidence unlikely. Just how much did Lucia know about what had happened to Josie, she wondered as she printed off the pictures of Lucia.

Rose sent a text to Trixie.

Everything is prepped for tomorrow. I will be there first thing, but not back until the next day. Any applicants?

Three so far. All have good background experience and we've spoken on the phone. They can all start immediately.

Okay, great. Happy to leave the final decision to you Trixie. Just make sure they know it's temporary until September.

Will do. See you the morrow. Night.

Rose smiled at the last message. How things had changed since Trixie had first started her apprenticeship.

Rose thought about the story Callum had told her about the prank, Lucia, having had her heart broken by Ant. Heartbreak seemed an unlikely motive somehow. Whatever was behind it, did it support Callum's claims of the hold Oliver had over him?

Rose clicked onto the fringe festival website. Alice through the Fringe had not been re-cast and was closed. According to the website the play would return the following year with a new cast. The director had also posted his apologies for any inconvenience. It seemed an odd statement, incongruent with a real-life fact, that one of his cast had been murdered. Rose studied the pictures of the other members of the show. The actors playing Tweedle Dum and Tweedle Dee looked like the pair she had met after talking to the director. They had similar features and were older than the rest of the cast. Rose couldn't find their names credited anywhere else as actors or performers. Everyone else appeared credible and had several acting credits. She thought back to the conversation she had had with the director about Lucy and looked at the earlier map she had made. What was Lucy's connection and how exactly had it come about that Lucy ended up playing in a show with Josie? If Josie had been fine with it, did Josie know about Ant supposedly breaking Lucy's heart?

Like most people of her generation Lucy, as Lucia, lived her life fully online. And she also managed multiple social media platforms under her acting name, Lucy. Rose found out where Lucia lived, met friends for coffee and which pubs and restaurants she liked to go to in less than half an hour. She also found out that, in her role as wife of a professor, Lucia was delivering a talk at the Girton branch of the women's institute at 2pm. Rose planned to catch the 9.00am from Waverley at Haymarket, but the connecting train from Peterborough to Cambridge didn't arrive until

14.05. Rose wondered if WI meetings still began with the singing of "Jerusalem". She would miss the introductory remarks, but she would be on time for the talk.

Rose took on the role of Libby the reporter once more, as she charmed two upstanding elderly ladies into admitting her into the hall of the education centre where the Girton branch of the Women's' Institute meeting was held. Callum might not have rated her acting skills, but Rose quickly observed Lucia had the audience eating out of her hand while she talked about her dual roles, as wife and actor.

"Are there any questions from the room?" The chair, a thin plainly dressed woman, looked about the audience. Rose raised her hand.

"Libby Forest, local Echo. Umm, thank you for telling us about your life now. I am wondering, could you tell us about your earlier experience, as a model for the painter Callum Blackwater?"

Lucia's eyes narrowed as she looked out to see who had asked the question. She put her hand onto the lectern where she had placed the notes she hadn't, up until then, needed to refer to. Her face flushed slightly. "There was an old rumour circulating, malicious gossip mainly, that I was that model, but no, it's not true, I have never been a life model for any artist, and certainly not Callum Blackwater." Her voice was shrill, thinner than it had been before Rose's question. The question had had the unsettling effect Rose had hoped it would. There was no mention in any of Lucia's online postings about modelling for Callum and she wondered if the good women of Girton would have been quite so thrilled to have her as a speaker, if they had been aware of Lucia's earlier career.

The room started buzzing with stage like whispers and a few coughs. The chairwoman stood up, thanked Lucia for coming and announced that tea was now ready. Any further questions could be put to their guest in person, via one of the chaperones.

Rose smiled inwardly as she watched Lucia escorted from the stage by the chair and handed over to her designated chaperones. Two other smartly dressed young women offered Lucia tea, a slice of Victoria Sandwich, and scones.

The two elderly ladies who had admitted Rose earlier came over and with a steaming cup of tea and a plate of biscuits. They remained with her for the rest of the afternoon and Rose realised she too now had designated chaperones who had clearly been told to make sure she made no further contact with Lucia. There seemed little point in staying. Rose thanked them and made her excuses.

She was standing at the bus stop when Rose saw Lucia leave the building and step into the back of the black Daimler that had been waiting in the car park. She had seen the driver standing outside the car, but Rose hadn't paid him any attention. Rose watched the car until it passed the bus stop, wondering if Lucia would acknowledge her. But as the car purred past her it wasn't Lucia that Rose fixated on. It was the familiar face of the driver. Rose cursed herself and then called a taxi, she knew it would be impossible to follow the Daimler by the time the taxi arrived, but chances are Lucia was on her way home to

Grantchester. If Rose was right, from the size of the property, the driver would be living there as well.

Vicarage Drive was one of the most expensive in Grantchester. So much for supposedly poorly paid professors and actors, thought Rose as the taxi parked opposite the impressive property where Lucia and her husband lived. The Daimler was still in the driveway but there was no sign of either Lucia or her driver. Rose peered out from the taxi window. She knew that the chances of being unobserved were slim if she tried to slip into the property during daylight. There was no B&B nearby but there was a local Inn that had rooms. The Inn wasn't one of Lucia's listed places, even though it was close enough to be a local. Rose hoped the driver might make an appearance at the bar. According to Lucia's social media post, she was hosting a dinner at home later. Rose noticed no guests had been tagged in the post, but she assumed Lucia's driver wouldn't be needed.

Rose paid the taxi and timed the brief walk between Lucia's house to the Inn. It was just before five when she checked in. After a quick freshen up she took her place in one of the small nooks opposite the bar. From there she could see both entrances and the door to the restaurant. She didn't have to wait long, his voice, the tone and accent announcing his arrival made her jump, spilling her lemon tonic water.

"Hello Bill, pint and a pie please mate."

Rose brushed her wet blouse and looked up as the driver took his place at the bar. The last time she had heard that voice was Terpsichore. The landlord nodded. "Be with you in a moment Jack."

Rose hesitated, she couldn't use her reporter disguise to talk to him, because she had booked in as Rose and she doubted pretending to recognise him as Tweedle Dee from Edinburgh Fringe would wash and she hadn't seen the play. It was a gamble he wouldn't recognise her from the day she had met the play's director, but she doubted he would. Most people didn't pay a second glance to someone walking through a door.

Rose sidled up to the bar, next to Jack. "Do you recommend them then, the pies?"

Jack turned to look at her. And, as Chris had done, two weeks earlier, his eyes demonstrated he liked what he saw, as he downed the pint. "Yeah, they're not bad, homemade at least. Haven't seen you around here before."

Rose smiled. "No, I'm just having a couple of days away."

"Right, well welcome." He put out his hand towards Rose. "Jack. Want to try one then? My treat."

"Rose," she said, accepting the handshake. "Err no thanks, unless they do a vegetarian version."

Jack frowned, the irony of her question and answer wasn't lost on him.

Rose smiled and coquettishly put her head to one side. Flattered by what he assumed had been a pick-up line, Jack's peacock feathers were immediately on display.

"Mind if I join you?" he said, nodding his head in the direction of the nook where she had been sitting.

"Watch out for this one Rose," said the landlord winking as he delivered Jack's second pint.

"Thanks for the heads up, but I'm a big girl." The two men looked at each other and then back at Rose's slender body before nodding to each other. Rose felt sick as she watched their ritualistic nudge nudge body language, bonding over what they assumed was on offer.

"I'll be back in a tick," she said and made her way to the toilet. Rose could feel the two pairs of eyes still ogling her as she left them. "Shape up Rose," she said sharply to her face in the mirror. "You're going to have to play him if you want to find out more and get inside that house."

When she arrived back at the table Jack had ordered another pint and what looked like a gin and tonic for her, "Bill said you were just on the tonic, so I cheered it up for you. Is that alright?"

"Normally, that would be my tiple, but I'm on this stupid medication, I'm not allowed to drink on it, or I'll pass out. But hey, who needs booze to have fun." Rose gave him a broad grin and hoped he'd swallowed her story. She dared not even have a sip if her plan was going to work.

"That's a pity Rose, but no problem. Maybe you're right. Who needs booze?" he said as he tipped back the rest of his second pint and started on the third.

Bill came over with the pie for Bill and a plate of salad with bread and cheese for Rose. "Sorry, nothing hot in the veggie line, but my wife made this ploughman salad for you. Alright?"

"It's perfect. Thank you, well thank her and can I have just a slimline tonic please, on my tab." Rose said as she pushed the gin over towards Jack. "I'm sure you can manage this."

Jack grinned. "Ooh Bill, I think she's trying to get me drunk," he said and made a clumsy grab for her.

Rose looked up at him, aiming for Princess Di, under the lashes, coy. "Not here," she whispered and put her hand on his upper thigh.

"Right you are m'lady," he whispered, loudly enough for Bill to still hear and pushed his tongue into her ear. "You're smashing Rose, did you know that?"

Rose bore the wetness and estimated how much more alcohol she needed to get the better of him. He wasn't a big man. The three pints and the gin he'd drunk in quick succession already seemed to be having an effect, but now he was eating she knew he'd need more.

"So, what do you do Jack?" asked Rose after she discreetly wiped her ear and spun him her story about teaching.

"Bit of this and a bit of that." I work for one of the big houses, driving mostly.

"But you're not driving tonight?"

"Nah, the lady of the house is having guests over. But my guess, it's really only one she's interested in." Jack gave Rose a theatrical wink.

"And her husband?"

Jack laughed. "Well, what do they say, when the cat's are away and all that. I don't know, it's a weird set up, I wouldn't put up with it if I was him. He's more often not there than there and she has all sorts over. Like tonight, who knows where he is."

Rose paused. Was Jack playing her? His answers seemed too pat for someone he didn't know. Not exactly the devoted and loyal employee she had expected, given his role in the play, which she had assumed was at Lucia's request. Had he recognised her after all? Had Lucia found out who she was somehow and sent him to meet her?"

"Tell me more. Although, should we go somewhere a bit more private, I mean I don't want to get you in trouble if someone's listening."

Jack smiled and leaned over to kiss her cheek. He finished the fourth pint and Rose ordered him a tequila chaser. "You're a Goddess Rose," he slurred.

Rose signaled to Bill for a double repeat order of drinks and asked for a tray.

"I'll bring them up love, you might not get him upstairs without a hand."

Rose nodded and slipped her arm through Jack's. Relieved he had turned out to be such a lightweight. As soon as Jack saw the bed in the middle of the room, he made a dive for it and beckoned Rose. "Come on dahlin.'"

Rose nodded and went to fetch the tray of drinks from Bill, who was already tapping on the door. "Let me know if you need anything else, Rose," Bill called over his shoulder, making his way downstairs.

"Rose, where are you?" Jack called out to her. He was unbuttoning his shirt and laying across the bed.

"Here, have a little sip while I get ready for you." Rose put the drinks next to the bed and propped Jack up with the pillows."

It was when he sat up, and the shirt fell open that she saw part of a tattoo on his upper chest. It was a swastika.

"You OK Rose, come on, stop messing about." Jack grabbed her wrist and tried to pull her down next to him."

"Oh, don't rush things Jack. Pleasure is much better when it's done slowly. You know that right, a big strong man like you." Rose whispered, her voice low and sultry.

"Yeah Rose, yeah, whatever you say babe," he said, knocking back the shot. "Slowly," he repeated, "slowly ..." His voice faded, as his head fell back onto the pillow.

Rose stood still, hardly daring to breathe as she waited to see if he would wake back up. But the next sound was a deep snort, Jack's mouth opened, and he rolled onto his side.

Rose knew she would have to work quickly. She pulled back the shirt to look more closely at the tattoo, before covering him with the sheet. The house was a ten-minute walk from the pub. If Lucia was entertaining in the way that Jack had intimated, it should be easy enough to search downstairs for whatever it was she hoped to find out. Rose took the keyring from Jack's pocket and put it in her own. Then she looked through his wallet. Jack Grimshaw was thirty-five, according to his driving license. There were three credit cards with different names and another license in the same name as one of the credit cards. The picture was different, but there were certain features, very similar to Jack's. A brother perhaps, or a cousin, had he been the other man at Terpsichore with Jack, when it was set on fire? Rose tried to recall the face of the other actor that had played Tweedle Dee. The two faces had blurred into one. Rose photographed the licence and the cards and slipped them back into his wallet.

The stairs from her room led directly down to the bar area. There was no way she could leave the Inn that way without someone noticing. Rose opened the window. Her room was at the side of the Inn and she wished she had thought to do a recce outside earlier. There was a large bush underneath the window, but she didn't want to risk jumping into it. She threw her backpack into it and paused. Jack was still snoring and no one outside the pub seemed to have been bothered by the rustling. There was a lower ledge, just out of reach. It had been a long time since she had trained to jump and fall but Rose trusted her muscle memory. She made the leap in faith and managed to drop squat from the ledge, down onto terra firma.

It was a half moon and Vicarage Drive was not overly bright as Rose made her way to Lucia's house. There was a light behind the window at the top of the front door and the central window on the upper floor was also lit. Rose assumed that was where the stairs were. The front downstairs rooms were dark. She knew from Jack's description of the house that the master bedroom was at the back, with views of the river. There was a small convertible in the driveway but the main gates to the front of the house were closed. Rose clicked the fob on the keyring, the gates remained firmly closed. Rose didn't try the key pad, even though so many people still used one two three four, she didn't want to risk setting off an alarm. She walked past the house and ducked into a shadowed crevice between Lucia's house and the adjoining property.

Lucia's house had six-foot railings on all sides, the neighbouring house had a low stone wall set next to the railings. Rose jumped over the wall and crawled on her belly towards the front of the two houses. Standing on the wall Rose pulled herself up between two of the rails, balancing her feet on the narrow strip, before taking another leap of faith onto grass and upsetting a flock of ducks sleeping by the ornamental pond. Rose lay still on the ground until the ducks settled. No one appeared, but a motion sensor light came on, shining across the landscaped garden. Rose waited, then crawled slowly back towards the fence, which was still in shadow. Jack had said his room was in a staff suite at the back of the house. The other two staff who lived on site were both away, Lucia was managing with a daily woman and a gardener.

While Rose made her way up the side of the house a young deer scampered across the back lawn. Another auto sensor flooded the back of the house with light. She froze as she heard an upstairs window at the back of the house open.

"You see, I told you, just wildlife, not your wife you silly silly boy." Lucia's voice rang out, cutting through the silence. "Come here, I'm not finished with you yet."

Apparently Jack hadn't been exaggerating about Lucia's appetite for extracurricular activities while her husband was away. So much for the dutiful wife she had played out in public earlier.

Rose unlocked the door to the staff suite and found herself in a narrow corridor with doors on either side and made her way to the door connecting the suite with the main house. The door was unlocked and unlockable. She wondered if Lucia's appetites extended below stairs. Was that one of the reasons Jack had been in Edinburgh with her, apart from thuggery and arson. Rose was about to cross the floor of the main hallway when she heard voices, then footsteps on the stairs.

"Oh for goodness sake, why are you behaving like this?"

"I'm sorry. I shouldn't have come. Just leave it will you."

"Oh, go to hell. I've got other fish to fry anytime I want. Leave now and there'll be no invitation back."

"I wouldn't accept one. It's not worth it, go fry your fish. Goodbye Lucia." With the ungallant comment hanging in the air, the man pressed a switch and let himself through the front door. Moments later she heard the car in the driveway roar away.

Rose waited to see if Lucia would come downstairs, instead she heard an almighty crash as Lucia let rip her temper on whatever she could throw. Rose stifled a laugh at the ironic contrast of the composed cool Lucia standing on the stage in Girton and the now rampaging and scorned childish Lucia throwing things across her bedroom, as the crashing noises above her head continued. She checked her phone for the time. Jack should still be asleep, but she couldn't risk being too long. Rose crossed the hall to the main sitting room. For someone with so many staff Rose was surprised at how untidy the room was. She found Lucia's office just off the sitting room. It too was messy, the elegant furniture strewn with boxes, papers and other detritus. Rose flicked through some papers on the top of the desk, they appeared to be a script for a commercial.

She opened the drawers and found various invitations, mixed in with photographs of Lucia with friends and Sam. The man Sam was with, was elderly, at least thirty or forty years older than her. The other drawers were full of bank statements, cheque books and receipts. Rose flashed her torch back over the invitations, she was about to close the drawer when she recognised the lettering on the top of one of the invitations. B U E with a swastika on either side. The invitation, dated June the previous year was to a dinner in Zurich, it had been hosted by someone called Olifer Hoffmann. Rose photographed the invitation. Rose checked her phone for the time and stole carefully back across the hallway, to find Lucia's husband's office. Jack had said it was on the ground floor at the front of the house. The sounds from upstairs had died down, and Rose could hear water running. There were two doors, the open door led to an elaborate dining room. The other door, closest to the front entrance, was locked. Rose opened her backpack and took apart a biro. She pushed the nib through the hole in the centre of the lock and waited for the click, keeping her head half turned towards the stairs in case Lucia appeared. Unlike his wife, Lucia's husband had left nothing on the top of his desk. The whole room was devoid of clutter or decoration of any kind, with the exception of a large, framed group photograph hanging opposite the desk. Rose had examined the picture - she didn't immediately recognise anyone, except for Lucia and her husband, but she photographed it for later anyway. Every bit of paper was filed neatly and everything inside the drawers was orderly, except for the stack of letters postmarked Canada, addressed to a Miss Summer Yeo. Devon's sister? She paused, she didn't have time to read them here. Rose put the letters in her backpack and crept back through the staff suite. It was just past midnight when she arrived at the Inn. She hadn't expected the Inn to be locked when she'd made her plan to drop Jack's keys at the bottom of the stairs inside. She fiddled with the set of keys Bill had given her earlier, and put Jack's keyring at the side of the stairs. Rose hoped Jack would believe he had just dropped them there, everything else depended on how much he remembered about last night when he finally came round from his alcoholic stupor.

Rose walked to the edge of the village and phoned for a taxi. The first train back to Edinburgh was not until 6.30am. It was going to be a long night on a hard waiting room bench.

Chapter Fourteen

Rose was on her third cup of coffee by the time the train arrived at Peterborough.

She had drawn and redrawn the map she started, whilst she waited for the first train out from Cambridge. Thanks to the picture in Lucia's husband's office, she had managed to connect several missing links together. But of course evidence and being able to obtain proof for her theory - as DCI Chatterton would no doubt remind her - was another matter altogether. She left him a voice message.

"I'm sending you some pictures, and some links to online sites. Are you free to meet me so I can explain what I think it all means?"

Then she sent a text to Trixie.

On the way back. Hoping to meet with DCI Chatterton. Will contact you when I know my plans. Let me know how things are going.

She made a legend for the map, at least her latest theory was backed up by some solid looking research. Rose had gone back to the original article she had first read by the journalist who found Ant and who had been at Terpsichore. Rose hadn't noticed before but the article the broken link was supposed to bring up was credited as belonging to a student from St. Aidan's journalism programme. If only Rob and Tod had talked to the journalist when they had seen her that day, at Terpsichore. After five murders, and so many lies ... Rose hoped what she had managed to put together would be enough and she knew the reality, getting international arrest warrants and working through Interpol was complex and difficult. Rose stared out the window at the passing countryside, and was almost asleep when her phone rang.

"Rose?" A woman's voice at the other end of the phone demanded.

"Sorry, who is this?"

"Alison Parks."

"Alison Parks the journalist?"

"Yes. Chris gave me your number. You're the fabulous Rose right?""

"What?"

"Tallish, beautiful, androgynous. That sounds like you?"

"Well two out of three I'll admit to."

"Oh I hate modest women, I really hate them. Have you seen what really ugly is? You should check out my profile?"

"Alison, It's been a long night and I'm not in the mood for banter. If you say that in the US. Your byline states that you are an American on the loose in England."

"I am American, but I work here, well in England, not so much Scotland. Why are you pretending to be me?"

"Sorry, what are you talking about?"

"You went to a meeting yesterday, where Lucia was speaking. You said you were a journalist."

"I wasn't pretending to be you. I didn't even use the same name, I was on the spot and then I said journalist. I've just been reading everything you have written about Oliver Moorcroft. How did you know where I was?"

"I was also at the meeting, your question stole my thunder."

"Oh, I am sorry about that."

"So you finally figured out the tangled web, who Nigel Foley aka Oliver Moorcroft is. Chris figured you would."

"No, well not until last night. How did you know?When did Chris realise?"

She heard a sigh at the other end. Then silence.

"Hello, are you still there?" Rose checked her phone, she was still connected to the call. "When did Chris give you my number?"

"Just before he was killed. Chris trusted you, but he also wanted to protect you. That's why he didn't tell you everything. We both wondered ..."

"What? What did you wonder? How did you know Chris?"

"St Aiden's, I used to give talks about journalism there."

"Is that where you met Josie too?"

"Yes. She would have been one helluva good reporter. Are you back in Edinburgh?"

"No, I'll be there in about ninety minutes."

"OK. Look, we should meet. I think you have figured out the information that would be helpful for the story I'm trying to put together about what happened to Josie. It's connected to the story that I'm hoping will come out tomorrow. Chris sent some of the proof I needed to publish that story in the newspaper. The editor won't budge without seeing the evidence. I'm just about to go live with an online article. It's click bait, but it will make a splash, driving my readers to what's coming. Then I'll pick up what Chris sent me and show the editor. But I need to do something else first. Check out some ferry passengers."

"Do you mean Callum Blackwater and Sam?"

"Yes. How did you know?"

"Callum came to see me. He said Sam was helping him."

"Oh yeah, she's helping him alright. Look I can drive up or we can meet halfway. Where are you now?"

"Oddly enough Newcastle is my next stop, we're just pulling in. I'll get off."

"Stay at the station, there is a buffet on the side your train stops at. I'll be there as soon as I can."

"Alison?"

"Yes."

"Nothing, I'll ask you when you get here."

Rose checked her phone as she made her way to the buffet. Nothing from DCI Chatterton, just a cheerful text from Trixie and Rob, reporting a successful first shift for the new hire. Rob was offering to bring her over some food later, when she was home. Tod was apparently a great vegetarian cook and *you would just love it* the text said.

Rose pinged back the joint reply.

Thanks, you are both due a bonus!

She desperately wanted to tell them where she was, about last night, but she knew she had to keep them out of it. The Edinburgh Fringe Festival hadn't worked out the way she had planned yet, despite everything, the shop and the stand were still solid. Rose knew the credit went to Trixie and Rob for the way they had backed her, stood by her, even when she had been at her most difficult. She went to freshen up in the ladies room.

"Time to smarten up Rose," she told her face in the mirror. "Be honest with them, they deserve that." She stared at her reflection. Her blind eye wasn't obvious, but the one that was failing had worsened in the last three months. How close she had come to going under and drinking again scared her. "Misery loves company," she reminded herself. Was that why she had agreed to be with Sarah, or turned to Chris for comfort? Neither of them were what she needed. She needed friends, her father, if she could figure out how, but most of all she needed to stay positive and not take one day at a time for granted.

She had already been at the station buffet for over an hour. The ferry terminal was about half an hour from the station, and Alison had said she was stopping by the newspaper offices. Rose, somewhat wired from all the coffee and lack of sleep, was getting restless, when a local news headline flashed up on the television.

"What the ..." said Rose as the headline moved onto the next item. She googled the name Alison Parks into her phone. Twitter and social media were on fire with Alison's name and references to the story she had posted online that morning.

Alison Parks in hit and run, outside newspaper office.

Alison Parks fighting for her life after a road accident.

Rose hit her fist against the side of the table. This couldn't be happening.

"Are you alright love?" asked the woman at the next table.

Rose nodded, realising the impact her outburst had had as a sea of faces stared at her. "Sorry." she muttered and scuttled out of the buffet, using her arm to wipe away the tears streaming down her face. The next Edinburgh train was in fifteen minutes. She hesitated. Alison had said Chris had sent research to the newspaper offices. Had she seen her editor before the accident, or were the papers still there, unopened? She called DCI Chatterton, but he was still not answering. She fished in her bag and found the DI's card.

"This is Rose McLaren, I'm in Newcastle. The hit and run, that journalist Alison Parks this morning. It wasn't an accident, I'm sure of it. She was on her way to meet me. Chris Foley, he had sent something to her that proved whatever she was writing was true, she was going to show it to her editor, so her story could go ahead."

"Slow down Rose. What are you talking about?"

"I put together some information, sent it to DCI Chatterton, but he hasn't come back to me about a meeting, so I can explain everything. I was on my way back to Edinburgh when Alison Parks, a journalist, called me. We arranged to meet in Newcastle. That was an hour and a half ago. She told me Chris Foley had sent her some information. Now she's, well, I don't know exactly, but it sounds as if she's close to death."

"OK. Rose, I'm just out of a briefing. I don't know anything about an accident in Newcastle. Why don't you call the police there, they'll be the ones to look into it."

"No, don't you get it? This accident, so called. It's all tied up with the murders in Edinburgh, Terpsichore, that girl's body you found."

"Rose, I don't know exactly what you think DCI Chatterton and I do, but let me tell you something he should have told you a long time ago. We get paid to investigate crimes, you're a member of the public and information is welcome. But putting two and two together and making five and interfering, maybe even putting an investigation at risk, and wasting valuable resources, that's not welcome Rose. That's not welcome at all."

The line went dead. Rose stared at the screen. If the DI wouldn't listen and whilst the DCI remained unavailable, she had three choices. To go back to Edinburgh, go to the hospital, or go to the newspaper offices where Alison worked. She chose the newspaper offices. The police were still outside, there was blood on the road and someone with a camera was photographing the scene from different angles. Rose paused, wondering if she should pass on the information about her planned meeting with Alison to one of the non-uniform police. But her experience from the call with the DI did not fill her with confidence that what she had to say would be taken seriously.

"Sorry, the editorial team is in a meeting right now. There's been a horrible ..." The girl behind the desk sniffed back the tears.

"I know, I'm so sorry. Alison was on her way to meet me. That's why I need to talk to her editor. I may have some information that will help. Tell him it's about the story Alison was hoping to publish tomorrow."

The girl nodded slowly. Her face was pale. She was young, and Rose realised it was probably the first time she had been faced that closely with something so horrible.

"It's alright, I know I have put you in a difficult spot because you've been told not to disturb them. But really, I can help, if you'll just let them know. I'll tell them I made you."

The girl picked up the phone, whispered into it, then nodded. "He's coming," she said quietly.

A few minutes later a tall thin man in his late fifties with a sallow complexion peered his head through the door. "Rose?"

"Yes."

"Follow me." He led her to the back of the newsroom into a small glass enclosed office. His desk was covered in files and papers and the computer was on a separate desk at the side. It was connected to the live news feed. "So?" he opened his hands. "What do you have to tell me that can help?"

"Did Alison see you before the accident, or was that afterwards?"

"The accident was before our meeting. Why?"

"In that case we need to find something that she was sent, the information, evidence to back up her story she wanted to show you."

"Gloria, come in here will you."

A matronly woman appeared, as if by magic.

"Look on Alison's desk. Bring me any mail, or a delivery. How was it sent?"

He looked at Rose.

"I don't know, but probably it would be from Edinburgh."

"I'll look," said the woman.

Neither Rose or the editor spoke while they waited. Aware of the ongoing speculation that the news feed was offering about the accident.

"Sorry boss, there's nothing on her desk. I've asked at reception and the mailroom, but ..." she shrugged.

"Ok, well keep on looking please. It has to be here somewhere."

Rose took the map she had drawn earlier from her bag. "Does this make sense to you?" she asked. "Is this what Alison was writing about?"

He stared at what Rose had drawn and then the legend. "How did you know?"

"I don't think I know everything, but this picture," she showed him the image of the picture she had taken in Lucia's house.

"Oh my God, where did you find that? Alison's been trying to find a photograph like that everywhere. I didn't believe her, I'm afraid. That's why I need proof, before I approve the piece. It's a huge scoop for her."

"Is this enough?"

"The marriage certificate would be better, but yes, I think it is enough. Can we use it? We will credit you."

"You can use it, but don't credit me, please. I think that would put me in harm's way," she said remembering DCI Chatterton's words when he left to follow Nigel Foley from The Sheraton forty eight hours earlier. "It took me ages to spot it. It was only when I realised who she was, that I started to see similarities to other people in the photograph.

Olifer Hoffman, aka Oliver Moorcroft aka Nigel Foley, Sam, aka Gerta Hoffman, Lucia, aka Lucy and him, this man. I first met him as Will Colby, he was directing a show at the Edinburgh Fringe, but his real name is Arthur Hoffman. I think he is Oliver's cousin - from the notes Chris sent to Alison. When I met him, he pretended to me that Lucy had been forced on him in Edinburgh, to play the part of Alice and that after Josie's death she was upset, needed to go home. If he hadn't said Cambridge, I might never have made the connection between Lucy and Lucia after I met with Callum Blackwater.

I wondered why Josie would have become friends with Lucy if Lucy really had been Ant's ex-girlfriend and behind the pictures Callum took. But, of course, it was the other way round. Josie was actually investigating Lucy; she had no idea that Will and Jack, playing Tweedle Dee, were also signed up members of the sick cause the Hoffman family believed in. When Josie found out and told Ant, that became a death sentence for them both."

"You've lost me. Alison has been writing about Olifer Hoffman's connection to a plan for a Nazi resurgence and art fraud, using the persona of Oliver Moorcroft a respected businessman and supporter of the arts. And Nigel Foley - equally respected in a different field, one that gave him access to rare coin collections."

"Oh yes, I realise that. But when Alison and I talked earlier she knew that I had figured out the connection between why Josie, Ant, Devon and Chris Foley were killed at the Edinburgh Fringe. That's why she wanted to meet with me."

"Who is Devon, you didn't mention him earlier?"

"He was the first victim. Wrong place, wrong time unfortunately. I don't think he was part of the original plan until he met Chris Foley and found out that Chris was a professor at St Aidan's. He gave Chris a letter from his sister. I found two letters in a drawer in Lucia's husband's desk, they were Devon's letters to her."

"You'd better take them to the police. I can't touch them, or anything to do with an unsolved murder."

"I know. Is there an update on how Alison is doing?" Rose nodded to the news feed. It kept repeating news about the accident."

"I'll need to get over to the hospital. I'm her, well I guess family as she has none this side of the pond. And only an older sister in the USA now. She's been here for over twenty years."

"Really, she sounds, I don't know, just off the boat."

"Oh, yes, she's proud of her New York accent and attitude. It's been good for us having her here. And she's got a loyal online following."

"She published a lot of quite controversial stuff."

"And she's made enemies, but I never saw this coming. I'll do more digging about what could have happened to whatever Chris Foley sent her. Thanks for coming here Rose. Let's keep in touch and good luck with talking to the police about what else you've found out. I hope it will help them solve those murders."

Chapter Fifteen

Rose really wanted to take a short but deep sleep, when she got home. Despite being overly exhausted, her body had other ideas, even the hot shower hadn't worked. Instead Rose fell into a series of unsatisfying cat naps but every time she closed her eyes she saw disturbing images of knaves and jokers. There was no news on how Alison was doing or whether she would be able to speak to the local police about what had happened to her and no message from DCI Chatterton. Clearly, she was out of favour and she didn't doubt Donna's influence.

She was ready to give up, after being half awoken, this time by hearing herself letting out a loud snore, when she felt the wet cloth over face and a hand squeezing down on her throat. She opened her eyes with horror to find herself looking into the man's face bending close above her own. It was Jack.

Willing herself to stay conscious and fight the chloroform Rose reached out her left hand and smashed the brass reading light across the top of his head. She knew she only had seconds before he re-established his grip. With the skill of an Olympian she raised up her shoulders, tossed back her head and twisted her neck out from under his grasp. It may have been years since she received combat training but her instinctive response didn't let her down. Jack put his hand out for her leg, only to meet her foot hard against his nose. The chloroform pad was laying on the bed, she threw it behind her, then leaped over the bed towards the door. Jack made another attempt to grab her but she spun at him, another kick, this time to his groin and she was out of the room. The front door to the flat was open, she darted through it, and down the stairs into the street, looking desperately for a passer-by with a phone.

"Rose."

It was DCI Chatterton. She had no idea why he was suddenly there, but she blessed him for it.

"Whatever has happened?"

"Quick." Rose pointed up to her flat. The man's face at the window ducked from view as the DCI looked up.

"I saw him," he said, pulling out his phone and demanding immediate back up. Rose leaned over and threw up on the pavement.

In less than ten minutes two police cars and an ambulance pulled up and Rose watched from the front steps of her building as Jack, handcuffed and somewhat bloody, was helped into the back of a police car. The paramedic had finished taking her vital signs and was trying to persuade her to go to the hospital.

"I'm really fine, I think it was shock and the chloroform that made me heave, I just want to be here and I need to talk to him." Rose nodded in the direction of the DCI as she sat down on the steps outside her flat.

"Rose, what's happening," she heard Rob's voice calling over the general hubbub, as the paramedic finally left and the other police finished up what they needed to do at the scene upstairs in her flat.

Rob landed on the step next to her, with Tod and Trixie standing behind him carrying two boxes.

"What's all this?" She waved her arm at them.

"Vegetarian food, remember – Tod's cooked for you?"

"Oh no, I really didn't, but now I do. Thank you so much for being here. You are all exactly what I need right now." Rose leaned into Rob. Trixie put the box down and squeezed in on the other side of Rose. They sat silently, each comforted by the closeness of the other as Tod looked on.

"We need to talk, Rose. Sorry but I can't let this wait. A uniform will need to come in with me." DCI Chatterton said, breaking the moment.

Rose nodded. "Well can they come in too? I think they deserve to know what's been going on."

"Alright Rose. Let's all go upstairs and let your neighbours get on with their ordinary lives. I bet they wish you would have one of those too, Rose."

"What? Oh, I see. An ordinary life. Very droll Chief Inspector, very droll."

"Ay well whitever has been going on, ah want the whole tale telt Rose, dinnae even think ye can scamper around any corners," said Trixie as she moved the paperwork and maps and helped Tod to arrange the dishes on Rose's dining table.

"Before any tales, I need a statement from you Rose, about what just happened. Just exactly what happened tonight. Otherwise, whoever that was will be away. He's already demanded a solicitor."

The female uniformed officer copied down Rose's version of what had happened. Then the DCI directed her back to the station. "I'll be there in an hour. Tell everyone to sit tight until I get there."

"Alright Rose, now you can tell me exactly what all the messages and photos you sent me earlier are about. That's why I came over to check on you – and it is a good thing I did."

"But Callum ..."

The DCI held up his hand. "That's all in hand. You can thank the DI for that, after your tip about the trunk. Callum is safe and well, at a hotel in Harwich."

"And Sam?"

He shook his head. "Why don't you tell me what you know about Sam."

Rose pulled out her phone and pulled up the picture she had shown to Alison's editor earlier. "Did you take a good look at this Chief Inspector?" Rose asked as she handed the phone to Rob, Trixie and Tod.

"Who are they? It looks like a wedding." said Rob.

Rose nodded. "It is. They are who is behind killing Chris, Ant, Josie and Devon and Devon's sister – the girl at Terpsichore. Today they tried to kill Alison Parks – she's the journalist that Rob and Tod saw when they went to Terpsichore. And tonight, they tried to kill me."

Trixie gasped, "Rose, why dae ye nae listen?"

Rose looked down. "Shall I tell the story, or not."

"Sorry, Rose. Ay o' course, I ken. I shouldnae ha' ..."

"It's OK Trixie, Rose knows we all care. And I'm kind of *with* you, but I do really want to know." Rob rubbed Trixie's back as he spoke.

The DCI remained silent. He had an idea what Rose was going to say from what she'd sent him earlier, but he wanted to hear how she had pieced everything together. She had arrived at her conclusions before he had, despite what Donna had said to her. Donna's prejudice against her own sex getting in the way once more. If he hadn't persuaded her to take what Rose had called about more seriously, she might not have found Callum in time.

Rose pulled out the map and the legend she had made on the train.

"Tomorrow, the paper Alison worked for will reveal that this man, Olifer Hoffman, a pro-right-wing Nazi is also this man, Oliver Moorcroft AND this man, Nigel Foley. He has three separate identities. It seems to be rather a family trait - Lucia, or Lucy I think is his biological niece. Another family member is Arthur Hoffman, who I first met calling himself Will Colby - I think he might be Oliver's cousin. He was directing the 'Alice in Wonderland' play that Lucy and Josie were in. And then there's Sam - also known as Greta Hoffman when she is in Zurich - is married to Nigel, or Oliver if you like. They were married in a secret ceremony in Zurich two years ago. That's the reason for this photograph. If you look very closely at his image, you will see similarities to these two men," Rose passed around press clippings of Oliver Moorcroft and Nigel Foley. The images of the two men were distinct and different, one blonde with blue eyes, the other dark with glasses "This is how they appeared in public. Publicly, Sam was only ever seen with Nigel Foley, and Oliver was never seen with a specific woman."

"How can one person have so many lives?" Tod said, the others nodded.

"Well, as Oliver he lived in the UK, until recently. He was educated in America, where he had picked up a strong American accent. Nigel lived in New York and Olifer lived as a recluse in Zurich. As rich men with access to private planes, they could hide in plain sight when they chose and have as much privacy as they wanted, when they needed not to be seen. Or disappear entirely when they get caught with stolen coins!"

"So, what brought Olifer, or whichever one he was, to the Edinburgh Fringe?"

"I haven't figured out if he orchestrated bringing everyone together or if he found out Ant and Josie would be here. I'm guessing he's been waiting for an opportunity perhaps he realised Alison Parks had more on him than he thought. I mean it is odd when you think about all the right-wing protests that have been happening at the same time."

"Tod, remember when you told Rob about that so-called prank that was played on Ant?"

"Yes."

"I think that the only crime Ant had actually committed was that he was Jewish and had befriended Callum Blackwater. Callum's grandmother had worked for the

British government towards the end of the war as a spy. According to Alison's research, Callum's grandmother had unearthed secrets about Olifer's grandfather – who was JWB, the artist! The same one who committed suicide and destroyed most of his paintings. Olifer Hoffman only realised who the spy was when a newspaper article was printed with pictures of the survivors of that espionage group.

"Olifer wanted to get even - avenge his grandfather whose politics he revered. But because she was already dead, Olifer chose to get his revenge through Callum, her grandson instead. The DCI already has one letter to prove that Oliver Moorcroft was behind the prank, it was written by Summer Yeo the female student to her brother Devon. These two are from her brother, written to her, after she was already dead, begging her to contact him and their mother. I found them in her house." Rose pointed to a picture of Lucy.

DCI Chatteron scratched his nose, "Found them Rose?"

"OK, I stole them, but they had already been stolen. It's why Devon was killed, and why his death was different. It hadn't been originally planned like the others, so I guess putting the playing card in his pocket was an afterthought."

"So, who killed Devon?" Asked Trixie.

"It must have been either Sam, Jack or Lucy, because Nigel was giving a talk about coins in Glasgow that night, and couldn't have been in Edinburgh, but I don't know how they did it."

"I know how, but not who," said DCI Chatteron. "But what I am about to say must stay here. Agreed?"

Everyone nodded and then murmured. “Agreed.”

“It was an injection of insulin, in the ankle.”

“Then that would be Jack,” said Rose. I don’t know if he’s diabetic, but there was a prescription for insulin in his wallet.”

“Not necessarily, but I need to make a call. When did you see the prescription, Rose?”

“Last night.”

Whilst DCI Chatterton went into the hallway to make his call the others stared at the papers and map that Rose passed around.

“This is about so much more than what happened here in Edinburgh, and out at Callum’s house, but what happened here has touched each one of us,” she said. “I know you think I shouldn’t have become involved, but I’m not sorry I did. I am sorry for the way I went about it though.”

“So why were Ant and Josie murdered?” Sorry to be dense,” said Tod.

“No, you’re not. It’s because Josie was also doing some research on Oliver Moorcroft and through the university she had been in touch with Alison. Will Colby who was directing the play must have seen them together. It might have been him that killed Josie, but my gut instinct says it was actually Lucy. She was right there - dressed as Alice - and had access as well as motive and it explains why no-one saw anything. I think that was what Alison was going going to tell me when we planned to meet. She knew bits that I don’t know, and I knew bits she didn’t. She was doing a story about Olifer’s connection to the murders as well as the political stuff, but of course, she had no evidence. Chris told her to talk to me."

"Chris did?"

"Yes. That playing card, it was probably Chris who left it under my door. I think he came here to find me because he wanted to tell me what was going on. I just wish I had been here, or that he had gone to the police. The clue, it was too cryptic, that question mark over the queen's face. I didn't see the connection until I saw this picture of Sam wearing a red diamond brooch."

"Dae ah get this right," Trixie frowned, "Sae Devon wis killt with an injection of insulin in the ankle by Jack. Josie wis stabbed in the heart by Lucy. And Ant wis clubbed over the heed by Will Colby – who is actually Lucy's father?"

"Yes, I think so," said Rose. "I suspect that Sam was also meant to kill Callum on the ferry. Tie up loose ends. Then Oliver would have a permanent hold over all of them."

"Whit aboot the cards then? How did they all ha' a card tae leave with the bodies?"

"I think, because Oliver was calling the shots over all the deaths. Whether it was a red herring to put suspicion on Callum, or maybe just as a dog whistle to the Neo-Nazi contingent in town ... I don't know. But Oliver was the only one who had that deck of cards."

"So who murdered Chris and why?"

"Yes, do tell Rose," said the DCI as he came back into the room.

"I am getting to that. The Dante book I gave you. What I thought were codes were really notations, look ... like these." Rose handed around a picture from inside the book and the legend she had made to go with her map. "It's Olifer's family tree."

"When Chris first talked to Alison, he didn't know that she was investigating his half-brother Nigel (aka Oliver Moorcroft). He also didn't make the connection between Callum and the fact that Oliver Moorcroft was the angel investor, until after he spoke to Devon – and just before Devon was murdered. Chris didn't really know Nigel that well – I suspect there was a good reason his mum never told him about having an older brother! They were staying at The Belvedere and that was when Chris saw the Dante book in Nigel's room. Chris was performing Dante, so I assume he picked it up and saw the symbols. I know that Chris had studied Egyptology and so he must have figured out the symbols had been used to spell names, a sort of family tree if you like. I suspect that's when he realised there was a connection between Nigel, Oliver Moorcroft and Olifer Hoffman and he stole the book. He must have been horrified to realise that Olifer Hoffman, a man who represented everything Chris hated, was his half-brother? He contacted Alison again, about the research she was doing and told her what he had found out. He promised to send her the breakdown of the code. That's what she was expecting at the newspaper office, not a marriage certificate, which was what her editor thought she was sending. Although of course Olifer had added his marriage to Sam (or Gerta) in the family tree."

"So, who murdered Chris, Rose?" The DCI held her eye, wondering if she was willing to admit she didn't know. How could she, it was a mystery. None of the players were in Edinburgh that night.

"It was Olifer, dressed as Nigel."

"Impossible," retorted the DCI, "He was in Chester."

"Remember what I said earlier, about hiding in plain sight. He was in full view in Chester, then, using a disguise, he took a plane to Edinburgh to meet Chris. At the same time, Jack, who is similar in height to Olifer, flew down to Chester. If you call the conference organisers, they will tell you that Nigel Foley had to withdraw from the afternoon's plenary because he had a tummy bug. And a member of housekeeping will confirm he was in the hotel suite all that afternoon, as will the guests who saw him from a distance while they attended the cocktail party at 7pm. I'm sorry to say I don't have written proof, but I do know, from a call I made earlier, that a private flight left Chester airfield bound for Edinburgh with one passenger on board. The same plane flew a different passenger back and arrived in Chester just after 2pm. According to the log, another plane delivered a single passenger to Chester at around 9pm. After the murder, when I asked you DCI Chatterton how Chris had been identified so quickly, you didn't want to say. But I thought, at the time, the only way would have been by private plane."

DCI Chatterton closed his eyes. Of course, she would have thought of that. He should have given her more credit. Rose had triumphed, and she had done so skillfully. Her attention to detail and capacity for looking beyond the obvious was something he wished many of his colleagues had. Her imagination was limitless yet, at the end of the day, she had always made sure the route on the map that she presented was credible, even when she couldn't prove it. He felt oddly proud of her. There was something about Rose that had kindled his regrets about being childless. If only her own father would see what he was missing by remaining absent from her life. He was about to tell her to call her own father when he felt a sharp pain across his chest.

"Are you alright?" Rose reached over to touch his arm. His face had gone deathly white, as he crumbled suddenly, into a heap on her floor.

Chapter Sixteen

Even though two months had passed, since August, the Fringe Festival seemed like yesterday to Rose. Her mind had been preoccupied ever since DCI Chatterton had been rushed to hospital with a heart attack.

It was late afternoon on All Hallow's Eve. The smaller children were already out guising. Muffins on Morrison looked spectacular, with painted ghosts and pumpkins adorning the door and window. Trixie's apple and cinnamon Murder Muffins, iced with ghosts and decorated with tiny headstones made from marshmallows, had sold out. Rose and Trixie dressed as ghouls with muffin hats were standing outside the shop, handing out free mini muffins and decorated shortbread when Rob arrived. He had spent the afternoon biking around Edinburgh dressed as a kilted zombie, offering treats and vouchers for the evening gig he and his band were playing at. The band had been booked frequently, following their success at Underbelly, during the August Festival.

"Och if it isnae the devil himself," exclaimed Trixie as Rob dismounted from the electric bike.

"Or is it the devil and his dark angels?" Trixie and Rose both turned to see DCI Chatterton, resplendent in a 1940's gangster style trilby hat, striped suit with a colourful walking cane coming towards them.

"How good to see you," said Rose, pulling out a chair from under the sitooterie table. "Here, park yourself down and I'll make us a brew, or would you prefer inside?"

The DCI waved away the chair. "No need for that," he said smiling, "but I'd love the tea, all the same."

"Ay, a''ll fix it, for ye, ye two have a lot of catchin' up tae dae," said Trixie as she disappeared inside the shop."

"It's good to be here, Rose. Thanks for your cards and messages. They kept me going."

"You gave me such a fright. I was so happy to get your message about meeting up today. Surely you're not going to go back to work yet though?"

The DCI didn't reply immediately. "I've decided it's time to hang up that particular hat."

Rose took a breath, so that was the mysterious news he had to tell her in person. "Haha, so you're going gangster now," she said, pointing at the trilby.

"Yes. That's me, from the good to the bad in one fell swoop." The banter was lighthearted, but Rose could tell, from the way his smile didn't quite meet his eyes, that here was not the place to talk. They hadn't spoken properly since the night Jack had attacked her and the DCI had been carried out of her flat on a stretcher. She had messaged, sent cards and he had texted her, but he'd been clear throughout, however much she prodded, he couldn't tell her anything about the investigation. He was out of the loop too.

Rose had given a statement to the DI, but Donna had ghosted her after that meeting. Whenever Rose tried to inquire what was happening, she was met with a blank wall of formality. The only thing she knew for certain was that Jack had been arrested and charged for the fire at Terpsichore. He was also facing further criminal charges for the assault on Rose, but there had been no information about when that was likely to be. The article Alison Parks had written, due to be published the day after her death, was never printed.

Callum Blackwater hadn't responded to Rose's calls or emails and there had been nothing in any of the other newspapers to suggest her information or hypothesis about Oliver and what had happened to Chris and the other victims during the Fringe Festival was being pursued or investigated. She had scanned the news daily for news of Oliver Moorcroft, but there had been nothing reported.

"Where do you want to have dinner? I haven't booked, I can rustle up something back at the flat, or we can go somewhere locally."

"Thanks Rose. There is something I want to talk to you about, and perhaps, given what's happened, it's more important than ever that I do."

"About the case?"

"No Rose. Sorry. It's about getting older, health stuff."

"Oh, of course," Rose tried to cover up her disappointment. "I just wish that ..." Rose paused, there weren't enough superlatives to describe what she wished without sounding churlish about what she regarded as the mishandling of all the information she and Alison Parks had discovered. She had felt dismissed and ignored but there was more to it than that, something more sinister. A cover up. But for what purpose? She even had her suspicions now that the playing cards were actually signs to someone high up in law enforcement to make those particular murders go unresolved. A deadly game indeed.

"One day Rose, one day it will all come out. You have to believe that." The DCI said, seeing the familiar thinking frown lines on Rose's face. He reached his arm out to her, the way she had done to him before the heart attack.

"If you say so," she straightened up and gave him a smile.

"I do Rose, I most definitely do. Now how about you and I go for that dinner, my treat."

"If you insist, that would be lovely. Thank you."

When all the mini muffins had gone, Rose locked up the shop and waved to Trixie and Rob as they headed off to get ready for the gig. Trixie in her role as number one fan of the band. DCI Chatterton, called to book a table for two at ViJay's - a favourite local Indian - and Rose was surprised to hear him book it under his first name, Anthony.

"DCI Anthony Chatterton, great name," she teased him.

"From now on, I'm just plain old Anthony Chatterton. If that's ok with you Rose.

"Sounds good. And Donna, will she mind you and me having dinner? I don't mean professionally, I thought you two had a bit of a romantic thing boiling."

Anthony Chatteron smiled, "Ah well, Donna found another fish to fry whilst I was poorly, not that I think it will last long, she tends to throw them back after a while. I'm too old for that sort of thing now. But no hard feelings and I would like her to be happy."

"If you say so," said Rose, putting her arm through his, as they walked to the restaurant together.

It was gone midnight by the time Rose was ready to turn into bed and reflect on their conversation. She would do as Anthony suggested, write to her father, try and reach out to him again.

Whatever happened, it was comforting to know that Anthony Chatterton finally approved and appreciated her machinations and oftentimes formidably stubborn approach to solving things.

Truth was important to Rose, and she knew in her bones that, for her, this was not the end of the sinister game that had been played. That she wouldn't be satisfied until everyone else, who needed to be, especially Sam, Olifer and Lucy were brought to justice. But just as she had waited for Troy to take his turn behind bars, she could leave it for now. She *had* figured it out and more importantly, Anthony Chatterton believed her.

Muffins on Morrison needed her attention, and she wanted to give Rob and Trixie a well-deserved break.

Scottish words used:

Aboot	About
Ah	I
Auld	Old
Awright	Alright
Aye	Yes
Baltic	Cold
Cannae	Cannot
Cos	Because
Dae	Do
Dinnae	Didn't
Doon	Down
Feart	Afraid
Frae	From
Guid	Good
Ha'	Have
Hame	Home
Havnae	Haven't
Heed	Head
Intae	Into
Jist	Just
Killt	Killed
Ma'	My
Mak'	Make
Mithering	Fussing

Mithering	Fussing
Movin'	Moving
Nae	No
Naw	No
Nowt	Nothing
O'	Of
Och	Oh
Oot	Out
Shouldnae	Shouldn't
Tae	To
Telt	Told
Th' morra	Tomorrow
Th' night	Tonight
Wasnae	Wasn't
Wearin'	Wearing
Wi'	With
Wid	Would
Wis	Was
Whit	What
Willnae	Won't
Womin'	Women
Ye	You
Yer	Your
Yersel	Yourself

The Festival Muffin Recipe by Amy MacDonald:

Instagram Food Blog - @amy_macdonaldeats

Ingredients

300g plain flour
1 tbsp baking powder
100g caster sugar
100g unsalted butter
2 large eggs
200ml semi-skimmed milk
150g fresh raspberries
100g white, or dark chocolate

Method

1. Preheat oven to 200C/400F/gas mark 6. Line your muffin tin with ten paper cases.
2. Sieve the flour and baking powder into a large bowl. Add the sugar.
3. Melt the butter. In a separate bowl, whisk together the eggs and milk. Pour the melted butter and the egg mix into the flour. Stir but take care not to over mix.
4. Stir in half the raspberries. Cut the white chocolate into small chunks and stir them into the mix.
5. Spoon the mixture between the cases. Dot with the remaining raspberries. Cook for 15-20 minutes until golden. Let the muffins cool a little before tucking in.

If you enjoyed

A GAME OF MURDER

You can keep up with Liza's latest news, follow her on social media and subscribe to the newsletter at:

https://linktr.ee/lizamileswriter

Liza's other works of fiction include:

- Murder on Morrison – A Rose McLaren Mystery
- Love Bites
- My Life's Not Funny

Printed in Great Britain
by Amazon